MASTER OF THE HUNT

A Bird Shifter Novella

MANDY M. ROTH

Blurb

———

Master of the Hunt
Book three in the King of Prey series.

When the oracle warns Prince Aeson that his future mate is in the human realm and is in great danger, he wastes no time going in search of her. Problem is, he has no idea who he's looking for. He's never met her and the oracle couldn't give him anything more than small clues as to who she is and where she might be.

Sent to one of his favorite hangouts—a sex club—Aeson is stunned when a beauty shows up on the arm of another man, a man void of emotion. He senses trouble surrounding her and something else— something that marks her as his. He doesn't care if she is or isn't the woman the oracle told him about, she's the woman he wants. Anyone who dares to stand in his way will feel his wrath and, before the night is out, she'll feel exactly what it's like to be taken by a prince.

King of Prey Series
_____

King of Prey
A View to a Kill
Master of the Hunt
Rise of the King
Prince of Pleasure
Prince of Flight

Dedication

To the fans of Kabril and the bird shifter realm. Thank you for embracing my rather odd imagination.

Chapter One

Accipitridae Realm, Buteos Regalis main castle...

AESON STEPPED BACK, allowing his nephews to run past him, each babbling about something he could not understand. Their father, the king and Aeson's eldest brother, chased behind them, appearing winded. In the nearly four hundred years he'd known him, Aeson couldn't recall a time when Kabril looked so unraveled. His duplicate in looks in every way, it was as though Aeson were seeing himself in such a situation.

The sight was sobering indeed.

"Kabril, you are showing your age," Aeson said, enjoying goading his brother as often as he could.

"I am two minutes older than you," Kabril replied. He motioned to his triplets, who were pushing the age of three. "I know naught how our father did it. Eight sons." He looked horrified by the idea. "They are my heart and joy, but brother, they never tire. It is the equivalent to one laying siege to the castle nonstop."

Chuckling, Aeson nodded. "So I see."

"Brother, the moons hold great pull over them. When the moons are full, I swear my sons sleep not."

Aeson laughed. Four moons orbited their planet. One of the moons was large enough to be seen during daylight hours. Often, the moons were attributed when madness, or in this case, too much energy came into play. "I do not believe for a moment they are subject to the moons' pull. They are merely young boys —fledglings—Kabril. We are old. They are not. It stands to reason they would have more energy than us. It is good to hear the sounds of children in the king-dom. For too long it was void of such noises."

Kabril motioned to the nanny charged with overseeing the boys before turning to face his brother. "No word of new births among our people has reached me. To date, only Rayna and I, and Sachin and his mate Paige have been successful. You know, Rayna believes we should consult the Oracle on the matter. She thinks it may provide valuable insight into what our next move should be."

Aeson cringed at the mention of the prophecy giving globe. From an early age he'd learned to both fear and stand in awe of the oracle's power. It was often consulted on matters associated with the gods or destiny. Kabril, unlike their father, wasn't superstitious. It made him a better leader in Aeson's opinion than their father had been, not that he'd been a bad one. "And I say you decree that all your loyal subjects must procreate like mad," Aeson said.

Kabril rolled his eyes. "Still chasing

skirts in the taverns throughout the realm?"

With a sly smile, Aeson rubbed his stubble-covered jaw. "Not in this realm, brother. I'm unsure a maiden exists here that I've not bedded. Earth is another matter altogether."

That caused his brother to stumble over seemingly nothing. "You? The famed lover of women of our kind and hater of all things human, now seeks out the beds of human women?"

"No. Not beds. But I do enjoy chaining them to walls and having my way with them," he replied. His cock hardened at the very thought of it. He did so enjoy women of all sizes and shapes. And he very much enjoyed taking them in different ways. "Did you know they have taverns or rather sex clubs, as they call them, devoted to that very thing? They rival our torture chambers and the women there line up for it, wanting to be punished by a man's hand before being thoroughly pleasured." He motioned with his hands, framing an invis-ible woman with exaggerated measurements. He then pumped his hips in midair, simulating fucking said woman.

"If my wife hears you speak of such things," Kabril leaned in, "and of demeaning human women in such a way, she will skin you alive. She may be human but she is something to be feared, brother."

Aeson tossed his head back and laughed. Rayna certainly was a fiery woman. She kept his brother in line nicely and brought out the best in him. He clasped his brother's shoulder. "Should I find one such as she, mayhap I would wish to chain her to my bed for I am not foolish enough to think I am immune to all women's charms."

"Do you not wish for a family, Aeson?" There was something off in Kabril's voice. "Do you not wish for love and happiness?"

He glanced in the direction his nephews had run off in. "I do not wish for such a thing." It was a bold faced lie. One he was sure his brother saw through with ease.

"Because you have no desire for one or

because you desire one so much that you fear it might not come true?"

His brother knew him well. Not only did they look much alike—nearly identical to those who didn't know them well—they tended to think on the same terms too. Though, Kabril had always taken things more seriously than Aeson had. Mainly because Kabril, as firstborn son, had to. Second to the throne in a family that was close-knit, Aeson saw no point in worrying over kingly matters when the odds of him ever having the throne were slim. Even Keonae, the youngest of the triplets, saw no need to trouble himself with the day-to-day trials and tribulations of running a kingdom. For reasons too dark to dwell upon, Keonae now resided permanently within the human realm—a place Aeson found himself drawn to more and more as of late.

Kabril entered the Great Hall and Aeson followed closely behind. Chains of gold hung suspended from the high ceilings. Open saucers with floating wicks were upon the ends of each, illuminating the vast room.

Aeson's brother took a seat on his throne. There was a reflective mixture in a bowl sitting to the left of the throne. Aeson knew it was used to help divine the future, something Kabril rarely did on his own, leaving the seers to do so for him.

Kabril eased back in his chair, his fingers skimming over the carved hawks in the dark wood. "Brother, it was not that long ago I found myself in your position. Wanting to deny what the Oracle had set forth for me."

"Good thing we have yet to consult it for me then, yes?" A nervous chortle broke free of him.

Pressing his mouth in a thin line, Kabril motioned for one of the attendants. "Bring the Oracle."

"What?" Aeson paled. "Kabril, no."

The attendants hurried off, nearly knocking over one of the suspended oil lamps in their haste to please the king.

His brother smiled. "Ah, it would appear you are too late."

Grunting, Aeson gave his brother a pensive look. "I have no wish to hear talk of things that may not come to pass. Worse yet, it tell me I'm to wed a woman with a hunched back or who is missing her teeth."

"Think it likely?" Kabril questioned. "We have such an abundance of them? We may not have many females in our realm but none are as you described."

He took in a deep breath, wanting very much to strangle his eldest brother. As the attendant returned with two of the priests and the globe of the oracle, Aeson crossed his arms over his chest.

The priest on the left bowed first. "Your majesty, you seek the Oracle's guidance?"

"No, follower of the path of the Epopisdeus," Kabril said. "My brother seeks its wisdom in regards to a mate."

The other priest gasped. "Such advice is frowned upon, my lord."

"Yet none of you hesitated to force my hand in finding a mate in that very fashion," Kabril reminded them. "You will do so for my brother."

"But, your majesty, what if the Oracle says he has no mate or that she once was but has perished?"

Aeson stiffened, his gaze locked on the white globe. He steeled his nerves and nodded. "Ask it. I wish to know regardless the outcome."

"Brother, you are certain?"

"Yes, Kabril. I am certain."

"Very well." His brother waved his hand dramatically in the air. "Priest, ask the Oracle."

The priests bent their heads, each humming and putting their hands over the globe. Aeson had seen it consulted enough to know no actual words were spoken. It was more a telepathic thing. The priests were seers—men able to connect with the oracle mystically.

The priest to the right turned his head towards Aeson. "It is most odd, my lord. The oracle tells us your mate is alive, but she will not be for long should you not find her."

His breath caught.

Kabril came up and off his throne, the smirk gone from his face. "What else does it say? Where is she? In what village does she reside? What does she look like? Her name?"

The priest to the left slumped his shoulders. "Your majesty, the Oracle responds in much the same way as when we ask it of other seers. It is vague. It is giving us only hints of it all, images, feelings, but they are short and incomplete."

"But that cannot be," Kabril said. "There are no female seers within our realm."

"Yes, there are none within our realm, your majesty, but legend speaks of seers born unto the human realm who are female."

Aeson still couldn't pull his mind from the knowledge his mate was alive but not for long.

His brother ran a hand through his hair, a nervous habit of his. "Aeson's mate is human?"

"Yes. It would appear so," a priest answered.

The other tipped his head, as if listening to the Oracle. "Sparrow? It is showing us the image of a sparrow. This means something important. It is representative of her."

"But how is it she can be a shifter and born unto the humans?"

"Your majesty, it does not present the image in that of a shifter form. It is simply a sparrow. No more. No less."

Aeson grabbed for the priest. "Where do I find her? She needs me."

"My lord," the priest said, trying to free himself from Aeson's clutches. "Please, we know not."

"Brother." Kabril broke Aeson's hold on the priest. "Priests, is there anything more you can offer him?"

"It is strange. The Oracle wishes for him to go to where he has been drawn to so much as of late. We cannot say why."

Aeson's eyes widened. "It wishes me to go to the sex dungeon, erm, club in the human realm?"

Kabril rubbed the bridge of his nose and the priests looked horrified at the idea of such a thing existing. "That is all. You may go."

They rushed off, taking the oracle with them.

"Brother, they are men who have dedicated themselves to the bird gods and who have forsaken carnal pleasures," Kabril said. "To talk of such a thing before them is unwise and cruel."

"And my mate is about to die," he answered. "I'll take the time to give a damn about the priests' celibacy when I know she is safe and well."

"I will gather men to accompany you," Kabril said.

Aeson shook his head. "This task is for me and me alone. Should I require assistance, I will send for it."

Kabril knew better than to argue the point. "Be well, brother, and may you find her healthy and eager to accept you."

Chapter Two

EARTH...

Aeson leaned against the wall of the darkened club and watched as the humans began their games. Music, or at least what humans claimed to be, played throughout the darkened club. He'd grown used to the pulsing sounds and beat—though much louder than music of his home realm. His people held tight to old ways. They clung to simpler ways of living rather than the human's need for more technology, more drama, more everything.

Once, many, many years ago, the two realms had been similar—granted humans had always lacked wings. When humans of yesteryear would catch sight of them, Aeson's kind was labeled gods, demons or even angels. Those were simpler times. Times when mankind could be warned away from pursuing who and what his kind were. With the advent of the internet, should one of their people be caught shifting forms and flying, there was a better than average chance the video would go viral.

That being said, there had been a point when there wasn't much difference between the two places. Now, humans referred to those years as the dark ages. They were anything but. They were a time when humans understood how precious and short their lives were and they lived them to the fullest. They did not hide away in their homes, speaking with others through varying forms of technology. No, they did so face to face.

Aeson's gaze traveled over the club once more. Some things had not changed much at all. Humans still sought out pleasures of the flesh—even with all their so-called advances. Soon enough the club would be what could only be called a giant orgy. It wouldn't matter that people would have paired off in groups of two or more. Everyone would be having some sort of sex and the debauchery would take place at the same time. Normally, he found the idea quite wicked and pleasing to his senses. Not tonight.

No, tonight he was anxious, wanting to be off and in search of his mate rather than here. The thought of countless naked bodies seeking pleasures from each other did nothing for him as concern for his mate flowed through his veins. Still, he stayed the course, believing the Oracle would not tell him to follow his pull to the club for no reason.

Would that it had given him something —anything more than vague hints and strange impressions. An image of her face would have been most helpful. Instead, he was left with nothing more than sparrows to go from.

Exhaling, he glanced at a young couple who were lying on one of the many sofas. They were opposite one another. The male lying one way and the female the other as they pleased each other orally. They held no concern for those around them—for the prying eyes, Aeson's included.

More often an observer than not, Aeson enjoyed watching the other club members sample one another. On occasion he'd permit one of the all too willing human women to suck him off as he soaked in the sights and sounds around him, feeling charged by the sexual energy in the air. Human women, much like the females of his realm, found him irresistible and wanted to please him.

A hard life indeed.

Being a prince is so difficult.

One such human woman approached, going to her knees and dipping her head. She lifted her hands, coming just shy of making contact with his thighs. She wanted permission to touch him, permission to unsheathe his cock and take it into her mouth. It wouldn't be her first time doing so. She seemed to crave the taste of his cock. He was not a man to turn down a good suck. He was about to grant her permission to do just that, when the air around him suddenly changed and a new sensation burst through him. Heat and then a wave of dizziness hit him. It took a moment for him to catch his bearings. He'd been alive nearly four hundred cycles and had never experienced anything such as this.

The Oracle's advice was not lost on him.

He visually scanned the club, desperate to find the source of the disturbance. Then he saw her. Light from the lobby area of the club spilled in behind her as a man led her into the establishment. Her lithe body had a fluid grace about it. Her blue eyes were wide with wonder and curiosity. They narrowed quickly as one of the waitresses at the club strolled past, clad only in leather straps and thigh-high boots.

Aeson stepped away from the woman on her knees before him and moved with determination in the direction of the newcomer, making it only a couple of paces. The sight of her siphoned the blood from all areas, causing it to pool in his cock. It hardened. The woman on her knees reached for him, her palms gliding over his cloth covered erection.

He caught the woman's wrist, his gaze never leaving the newly arrived beauty. It was she who brought his cock to life. She who demanded his attention. Her light brown hair was kissed with streaks of gold and fell to her mid back. She turned just a smidge and a breeze from the opening door ruffled her hair, her scent instantly finding him.

His body burned for the change. He wanted to shift forms—to allow his wings to sprout and to charge forward and seize what he wanted. The need to shift was great and growing at an alarming rate. He stopped, needing to take a breath and compose himself. It was hard to cage the animal side of him but it had to be done.

The breeze lifted her short blue dress, revealing a glimpse of matching panties. Aeson moaned and grabbed the chair nearest him, clutching the back so tight it began to splinter. He'd never responded this fiercely to anyone or anything. She had to be the one the oracle spoke of. She had to be his mate. But he needed to be sure. He needed confirmation.

The club's owner walked past and Aeson grabbed the man's arm, mindful of his strength. "That woman. Who is she?" he managed, just barely.

"The one in the blue baby doll dress?" asked the manager.

He nodded, unsure what he was agreeing to.

A baby doll dress?

The owner shrugged. "I don't know. I can tell you that guy she's with is a weird one. Got all jumpy when I told him I needed references for him to have his own room. Even tried to get me to take a huge wad of cash if I didn't ask any questions. I told him no references, no room. Really thought the asshole was gonna take a swing at me. Kept mumbling about a masterpiece or something. Anyways, his references told me he's a voyeur—likes to bring in girls of his choice to be fucked by another guy. The girl is a club regular normally, not someone he's bringing in too."

Aeson attempted to read the male with the woman in blue. One of his many gifts was the ability to sense intent. It had proved useful when weeding out traitors among them. While it was often hard to control around his own kind, humans were normally no matter. But the harder he tried, the blanker things became.

Curious.

The man's mind was dark.

Incredibly dark.

Almost void of anything.

The man in question yanked hard on the woman, jerking her through the mass of bodies. The fierce and unexplainable need to protect her came over Aeson and he was powerless to stop himself from charging forward.

———

SHELBY SPARROWS TOOK a tiny step back, no longer sure of her decision to attend a club with the man she'd been seeing less than a month. He'd seemed nice and normal. As he led her deeper into the thick of a club that she'd never heard of or would have ever gone to, she wasn't so positive.

"Roland, I don't know about this," she pressed.

Ever the suave one, he flashed a dimpled smile and continued dragging her through the crowded club. Just about everyone there was dressed in leather of some sort and many of them looked like they were answering a casting call for a dominatrix movie. There was so much exposed flesh that she couldn't believe her eyes. She wasn't a prude but this was a tad much.

"You told me this was a dance club," she said, trying to get her voice to rise over the pumping techno beat.

"What?" He didn't slow his pace. He moved so fast that he caused her to slam into what felt like a wall.

A very hot, very hard, very muscular wall.

She gasped as strong hands grabbed her sides, steadying her. Roland kept going, nearly ripping her arm from her socket.

She yelped and the same strong arms that held her, jerked Roland's hand free from hers.

"Hey," said Roland, stopping and facing her. "Shelby, come on. I told you that I have a surprise for you."

She looked up and had to step back to see the face of the man holding her. He was breathtaking. Men didn't come made like him. Dark brown, wavy hair hung just past his broad shoulders and eyes of pure gold stared down at her.

"Shelby, come," Roland demanded and she tensed.

The large man before her, dunked in leather from the waist down and wearing a snug fitting black, short-sleeved shirt, grunted. His attention went to Roland and Shelby couldn't help but notice the size difference in the men. Roland stood about six foot. The man in black had another half foot or more on him, not to mention much more body mass.

Much, much more body mass.

"Aeson!" another man shouted,

rushing up behind the guy in black. "Everything all right?"

The sexy man nodded.

Aeson.

That was an interesting name.

"Okay, if there's a problem, get me." He walked off, glancing back twice as if to see if something had arisen.

Roland either didn't notice or didn't care that Aeson looked like he was hoping for a chance to break him in two. Instead, Roland slipped past the man and plastered a saccharine smile to his face. "Shelby, sweetheart, I've been planning this for us for months. Come on."

Clearing her mind slightly of thoughts of the man in leather who seemed as glued in place as she was, Shelby looked towards Roland. "I'm sorry? Come again? Months?" She shook her head and let out a soft, nervous laugh. "You mean weeks, right. I haven't known you for months."

His light blue gaze lit with something that made her gut clench. "Isn't that what I said?"

She glanced around. "Roland, what is this place? It's not a dance club, is it?"

"People dance here," he said, still watching her in a way that made her throat tight. "They do whatever they want here. I thought you'd know that already. It's a place where your every fantasy can be realized."

A seriously bad vibe was coming off him.

Out of the corner of her eye, she spotted a woman being bent over a table, looking all too eager to have her red leather mini skirt pushed up and over her ass. The man behind her undid the front of his pants, seemingly unconcerned with the fact he was in a public place. As he withdrew his erection, Shelby's gaze whipped to Roland. "You brought me to a sex club?"

He schooled his face. "I'm surprised you realize that is what this is. You're so," he touched her cheek, "innocent and trusting. Like a little lamb."

Lambs to the slaughter.

The catch phrase she'd heard before

from a source she didn't want to believe was real let alone standing near her resonated in her mind. Fear and unease danced over her skin.

"R-Roland, I want to go home now."

"Nonsense, darling," he said. "The fun is only just about to begin. If this one is interested," he glanced at Aeson, "he's welcome to tag along. At least to start with. We can watch one of the shows and then break away to enjoy ourselves privately."

Her lungs refused to take a breath as she let his words sink in. In a sudden act of desperation, she reached out and grabbed Aeson's hand. He caressed her inner wrist and stepped in closer. "I will allow no harm to come to you and none will do what you wish not to have done." He paused a moment. "That includes the one which you arrived with. Should he push me on this, it will not end well for him."

His words while meant to be comforting worked both ways. She clutched his hand tighter. "I think I'd like to go home now."

"Very well," Aeson said, moving her

away from Roland and starting towards the door with her.

Roland reacted, grabbing her other hand. "Hold on. No. What I mean to say is let's stay for a bit, Shelby. I just thought this might be that walk on the wild side you mentioned craving."

She tried to calm herself down but something wasn't right. She found herself moving towards the man who was technically a stranger, while realizing the one she came with was truly the one she didn't know.

Chapter Three

AESON HELD THE HUMAN FEMALE TO HIM, every inch of him burning with the need to take flight with her. To whisk her away to his realm and keep her forever with him. She came to just under his shoulder —small compared to the females from his realm.

A shiver ran through her and he wrapped his arms around her, raising his core temperature to warm her. The man with her, whom she'd called Roland, gave Aeson a hard look, seeming as if he might actually comment. Sensibly, he kept his mouth shut.

"I have a private room for us, Shelby," Roland said. "This one can maybe watch a show or two with us and then come to our room for a few drinks, then be on his way."

If the male thought Aeson was leaving Shelby alone with him, he was wrong.

Dead wrong.

From the way she stayed close, Aeson suspected she too was beginning to sense something was very off with her male friend.

Patting his chest gently, she looked up at him, her blue eyes wide. She nodded. "I made up my mind. I want to go home. Please."

"Of course," said Aeson, dipping his head, her lips too tempting to resist a moment longer. They were the color of lacine berries which were native to Accip-itridae. He wanted to know if they were as sweet as the berries from home.

Anger rolled off her male friend in waves. Aeson turned her enough that he now stood between her and the man. A master and her slave picked then to stroll past. The master tugged at the collar the male wore and when he didn't respond fast enough, the woman turned and cupped his chin. "For that you'll spend the night licking me."

Shelby's sharp intake of breath was endearing, her innocence making him want her more. Normally, he sought out only skilled bed partners, having spent too many of his early cycles training the inexperienced.

"Shelby, don't be ridiculous," Roland blustered. "You were reading a book about this very thing not that long ago and—"

She went ramrod stiff and practically glued herself to Aeson. Not that he was complaining. Her ample breasts smashed against his chest, her nipples hardening at the closeness. They were like diamonds against him, hard, precious. The woman was bewitching. That was the only thing that could explain why simply having her near him left him on the verge of ejaculating.

"H-how do you know about the book?" she questioned, her voice barely above a whisper. "I don't think I'd have told you that."

Roland's expression was unreadable—

a sure sign a man was lying or at the very least, withholding information. "Of course you did. How else would I know? You've been under so much stress, darling. I just wanted to do something special for you. Something to help you loosen up."

Shelby relaxed slightly but remained close to Aeson.

Another woman he'd permitted the honor of taking his cock in her mouth approached. She set her sights on Shelby and licked her lower lip. A spark of jealousy ignited in the female's gaze and he knew he would not like what was about to happen. "Master Aeson, if you'll have me, I'm all yours tonight. I would love to serve you." She stepped closer, crowding him with her tempting body. "I can do more than you've let me even. So much more. Just accept me and I am your slave for the night."

As Shelby jerked away from him, he silently cursed. He clenched his fists. "No. I have selected another."

The woman's expression hardened on Shelby.

Shelby glanced at him and whatever she saw made her do a double take. "Oh, no. Not me. No." She paled as she took in more of the sights the club had to offer. A woman was in the process of being secured to a St. Andrews cross by two men in masks. All persons within the club were willing—aside from a very nervous and taken aback Shelby. Her jaw dropped. "You have got to be kidding me!"

Her outburst drew the attention of others.

Aeson hid his laugh as she cringed, almost darting back into his arms but stopping at the last minute. She pointed towards the woman on the cross in a delicate and discrete way. "That something you do too, Master Aeson?"

He knew he was being mocked and didn't mind in the least. Normally, he permitted only his brothers the luxury of such familiarities, but she was an exception.

Dipping his head, he put his face close to hers. "If you wish to be spread wide for

31

me, all you have to do is ask and I shall make it so."

She squeaked.

"Is it your wish?"

"No one is spreading me eagle on that thing," she replied, her voice shaky.

Aeson stood to his full height, pondering her statement. "I know of no eagle that can spread in quite such a manner. Close but not exact."

She stared at him.

Lifting his arms, he thought harder on her wording, attempting to mimic a move such as the cross would make. "I suppose it could be done."

"Are you on drugs?" she asked.

"Pardon?"

"Drugs," Shelby answered. "Are you on them?"

"No. Should I be?"

"What do your doctors say?" Her lips twitched as if she were trying not to smile.

"They tell me I am a healthy," he crowded her body with his, "virile man with an appetite for life's carnal desires.

They have told me to indulge in them. It is the only cure, so they say."

"You need new doctors."

The smile that spread over his face caught him off guard. Never had he enjoyed witty back and forth more with a woman. Each word that fell from her luscious lips was pure temptation, an invite to verbally spar with her before sinking deep into her.

"Should you find yourself changing your view on the cross, do not hesitate to notify me. I can tell you that I will be imagining you spread upon it all night."

Something akin to a strangled mouse cry came from her at his words.

Roland seized the moment to grab her hand in his. "Shelby, darling, this is a chance to live on the wild side. To walk the edge you crave."

"I crave chocolate not that." She thumbed towards the cross. "I don't even know what to call that other than painful. And I'm sorry, but I get these people are totally into this. That's wonderful but it's really not my speed. If I'm not comfortable being here, you, as my date for the evening, should be courteous enough to escort me home. After all, you drove, Roland."

She spoke with an air of superiority that made Aeson question her occupation and upbringing.

Roland seemed surprised by her stance. "Shelby, where have you been hiding this side? It's... exciting." He stroked her cheek tenderly and Aeson considered breaking the man's fingers one by one. "Do you have any idea just how beautiful you are? Take this fire in you now and live a little. Life is so short."

She seemed to think upon it before she glanced at Aeson. He inclined his head, willing her to understand he would not leave her side. Even if she wanted him to, he didn't think he could. Whatever was happening between them, it was on a baser level. One he had no chance of denying.

He didn't want to hope she was his mate. To do so and find out it wasn't true would be devastating, especially since she sparked such raw yearning in him.

Aeson put a hand out to her and much to his delight, she took it. He waited for Roland to be foolish enough to comment. He didn't. Instead, he led the way deeper into the club to a seated viewing area. Velvet covered sofas flanked by end tables were set up in various ways on what would normally be considered a dance floor area below the stage. The area was constructed to permit patrons to watch whatever show was being presented while being free to explore their sexual desires in a laid back setting.

Reluctantly, Aeson permitted Shelby to sit between him and Roland. He'd have preferred the poor excuse for a man sit on a different sofa altogether. He hid his delight as Shelby naturally slid closer to him rather than the man she came with.

Roland ordered a round of drinks and then touched Shelby's face, directing her attention to him. He kissed her and Aeson lost his battle with his self-control. He was about to seize the man by the throat, when

Roland stopped his kiss and twisted Shelby around. He cupped her chin and looked directly at Aeson. He nodded.

Aeson put killing the man aside for the moment, deciding instead to sample what he was offering. Hesitating above Shelby's lips, he waited for a sign she was willing to accept his lips on hers.

Her eyelids fluttered closed and she came to him, feathering her lips over his. The kiss was barely there to start with until Aeson took control. It was in his nature to dominate—to assume complete and total control of the woman. He watched for any indication of her wanting to stop but she gave none. She did however, run her hands up the length of his arms and into his hair. She moaned as he parted her lips with his tongue.

Her body trembled and he had to fight to be gentle and slow with her. She was so timid yet responded to him. He could smell her arousal and wanted to bury his head between her legs and taste it.

SHELBY SANK AGAINST AESON, her mind screaming at her for agreeing to stay and then for giving in to the urge to kiss him. Never had she felt like this before. So free. So liberated. So sexy. So totally out of control.

The way Aeson looked at her made her feel wanton. Like he knew under it all she could be as bad as any other girl. Vaguely, she heard moaning and light grunting. She paid no mind to it, her full attention on Aeson's mouth. God, the man was pure sin and sex all wrapped in a deliciously male packaging.

Hands that couldn't belong to Aeson ran up her sides before cupping the undersides of her breasts. She tensed and came to her senses, jerking free of both men, facing forward, refusing to acknowledge her loss of willpower. Unfortunately, the show had started and the grunts and moans were explained as Shelby found herself staring up at a woman artfully accepting two men into her body at one time. Her eyes widened.

Chuckling, Aeson leaned and pushed

her hair over her shoulder, his lips grazing her ear. "Fear not. I do not share what is mine and, Shelby, you most certainly will be mine."

Roland slipped closer to her, his hands roaming towards her breasts again. Aeson caught Roland's wrist, halting his progress. For a man who supposedly enjoyed watching, he was very touchy with Shelby and Aeson didn't like it one bit. He didn't even care that he was acting insanely possessive of the woman. Whatever was driving him felt right and he wasn't about to question it. He also wasn't going to permit any man other than himself to touch her.

She crossed her legs and the smell of her arousal hit him full force. A growl ripped free of him as his hand found its way to her bare thigh. She raised her leg enough that his hand slid under her short dress. The pounding of his blood rushing through his veins was nearly deafening.

Shelby sighed, touching her chest lightly. The sight of her fingers grazing her cleavage was too much. He made a bold move, inching his hand up higher, to her inner thighs. He half expected her to slap him and move away. When she touched his leg, her fingers skimming his erection, he grinned.

"Oh my stars," she whispered so soft a human couldn't hear it.

Aeson used his free hand to inch hers higher on his clothed cock.

Her cheeks flamed with pink and he dipped his head, wanting to taste of her lips again. She arched her back to him, her lips skimming his once more.

His cock twitched and she made another mouse sounding noise before lifting her hand from his inner thigh. She let it hover above his leg, her gaze locking with his.

"I shouldn't be doing this," she said. "Why am I doing this?"

"Because you feel it too."

Closing her eyes, she seemed so content as she rotated her head slightly. "It's like I'm..."

"Drawn to me?"

She kept her eyes closed. "Yes."

Roland eyed her and Aeson considered killing him just because.

"We should head to our room. Let me open your mind," Roland said.

Shelby gasped.

Fear struck Aeson full on and it took him a moment to realize it was radiating from Shelby. She let on no outward signs. If anything, she seemed to relax more, as if compensating. She stood and Aeson and Roland mirrored her actions.

She swayed, her gaze moving towards a coming waitress with a tray full of beverages. Timing it, she waited and then turned to Roland as she pressed a chaste kiss to the man's lips. The waitress collided with him, the drinks spilling everywhere.

Roland twisted and snarled at the waitress, bringing his hand back. Shelby grabbed it and tugged gently. "It's okay. Just go wipe up in the restroom and you'll be fine. No harm, no foul."

He dipped his head more, his mouth capturing hers. The growl that sprung free of Aeson was unavoidable.

"I'm so sorry," the waitress said. She

looked towards Aeson as if waiting for him to tell her what to do.

He inclined his head. "All is well. You may go." He focused on Roland. "I will watch over her. Go," he said, adding a push to his voice humans found difficult to resist.

Roland went.

The minute Roland was out of sight Shelby grabbed his arm. Heat flared instantly between them.

"Phone," she blurted. "I need a phone. And please don't leave me alone with him, and whatever you do, do not let him get you alone either."

He stared at her hand on his arm for what felt like forever, committing to memory the feel of her touch, before nodding and motioning in the other direction. No words were spoken as he led her deeper into the club.

Chapter Four

SHELBY PUT HER HAND IN AESON'S NO longer caring that he was some sort of sex god among these people. He was safe and she needed safe. He didn't object, moving through the crowd with ease.

Someone grabbed hold of her arm and spun her around. She brought up her other hand and struck out, palm first, hitting the person in the face.

"Ouch! Son-of-a-bitch, Shelby, it's me!"

"Panos?" It took her a moment to believe it was really him because he wasn't in his normal attire. In fact, he looked nothing like a detective. He looked like someone who was thoroughly submersed in the BDSM subculture.

He rubbed his jaw. "That hurt."

"What are you doing here and why are you dressed like… ohmygod, do not tell me you're into—"

A feminine laugh came from behind her. "Uh, no. Panos still blushes when he spots my cleavage while we're on a stake-out. It took some major arm twisting to get him in that outfit."

Shelby drew in a sharp breath as she spotted her longtime friend all done up as well. "Kim?"

Without waiting for an explanation, Shelby tossed her arms around her friend's neck and hugged her. "I was coming to call you and Shelton. He's here. It's him. The man you've been searching for. The Bondage Butcher. I didn't know at first. I couldn't see it but I feel it now and the things he's said they're—"

Kim held her out at arm's length. "Shelby, I need for you to take a deep breath. This place is crawling with our people and your brother is being restrained outside in a surveillance van."

"Sparrow is going to fucking kill me for this," Panos said. "He's been against this plan from day one."

"Sparrow?" Aeson questioned. "What is this of a sparrow?"

"Plan?" Shelby echoed Kim, ignoring Aeson a moment.

Aeson stepped closer to her and she instinctively moved towards him. Her palm went to his chest and his hand came to a rest on the small of her back. The act felt natural. He felt safe.

Panos was the first to speak, "Shelby, when you called Kim and told her the dreams stopped in the blink of an eye, she got a little concerned, especially with the number of threats this guy has leveled against you over the past eight months. Sparrow's done his best to explain how it is what you do works—that it doesn't work for you personally, that you can't read yourself or anything directly influencing your personal future."

"What is this talk of a sparrow?" demanded Aeson.

Shelby caressed his chest. "My last name is Sparrows. People call my brother Sparrow."

He gasped and jerked her against him. "You are her."

Kim locked gazes with Shelby. "You stopped having any kind of visions about the killings the very same day Roland bumped into you at the coffee shop and sweet talked you into your number. It bothered me. He bothered me. I'm sorry that I went to your brother about it, but my gut said it was the right thing to do."

"Her gut was correct," Panos said. "I put a detail on the guy and he's certainly suspicious." He cleared his throat. "He's been watching you for eight months. Learning your routine. He's got, umm, well—"

Kim rolled her eyes. "Sweetheart, he's got pictures of you through your bedroom window and the things he's done to the pictures would make you vomit. We were going to move on him last week, but nothing we had could hold up in court. The bastard has raped and killed seven women that we know of. We can't just let him walk."

"So you what?" questioned Shelby, sliding against Aeson more. "Decided to use me as bait?"

Panos closed his eyes briefly. "Shelby, you've been his next target for eight months now. He set his sights on you when the media reported you were assisting on the case. He fixated on what you can do. You know this guy better than any of us ever will. You've seen into his head. When he sets his mind to something, I think you know there is nothing that will stop him. I refused to risk moving on him without enough evidence because I won't watch that fucker walk out of the courthouse and then come for you like he's been planning all along."

"As much as Sparrow hates this, he knows Panos is right," Kim added. "Roland will walk right now if we move on him and he will come at you when we're not all there, watching over you from outside your place. We haven't let you be alone with him yet. One of us is always close, always watching. We knew he was planning this. It's why we're here. The owner of this place had some red flags shoot up and he didn't hesitate to call Panos. You think Panos wears a dog collar for just anyone? He loves you like a little sister and doesn't want you hurt."

"He's almost done washing off his shirt," Shelby said with conviction. No one questioned how she knew. "Don't ask me to touch him again. He put his tongue in my mouth and I almost threw up. I've seen what he does to women. I've gone on dates with this man. I've sat across from him laughing at his jokes and... oh God, I invited him into my home! Don't ask me—"

"We just need for you to let him take you to the room he prepared here. We won't let anything happen to you."

Tears welled in her eyes. "O-okay."

"Sweetie, don't cry. He can't know you're onto him."

Aeson wrapped an arm around her and pulled her close. "No."

"No what?" Panos asked, arching a brow.

"No. She will not do as you ask. If he comes near her again, I will rip his head from his shoulders and deliver it to you personally, but she will not be the bait you seek."

Shocked, Shelby looked up at him, still pressed close to his body.

"Excuse me but who the hell are you to tell us what she's going to do?" Panos crossed his arms over his chest. "You want arrested for obstructing justice?"

Aeson merely grinned as if being arrested by Panos was the most amusing thing he'd heard all day. "You could try."

"Why you—"

Kim intervened, moving between Panos and Aeson. "Shelby, I wasn't aware you knew anyone that hung out in places like this. Can you get your special friend there to back down?"

"Oh, no. I don't know him," she protested.

An odd look came over Kim before she licked her lips and wagged her brows. "You cling to strangers? Huh, interesting. I don't recall a time I've seen you be this way with a guy, especially one you only just met. And don't think we didn't notice you kissing him on that sofa."

Realizing her friend was right, Shelby released Aeson and took a giant step from him. She was about to head away, fearing Roland would get suspicious when the overwhelming feeling that someone she loved was in danger came over her.

She swayed and reached out, needing to steady herself as her vision blurred and her mind fogged, filling quickly with details of events she should, by rights, have no knowledge of.

Aeson was there, taking her arm, keeping her upright.

She opened her eyes and looked toward Panos. "Shelton. Something's wrong."

"He's being held back by three of our men but they'd never really hurt him,

Shelby. Sparrow's a legend among guys at the station. They all look up to him."

Pinching in her temple caused her to wince in pain. "Shelton."

"Shit, Shelby," Kim said, grabbing for her. "Sweetie, take a deep breath and I'll find you some aspirin."

"He's so tired," she whispered. "Long day. Longer night."

Panos grunted. "She can't do that whack job shit in here."

Kim slapped her partner. "That whack job shit has never steered us wrong yet and don't you dare take that tone about it or her. She's not crazy and the visions hurt her so shut the hell up."

"Tired," she repeated. "Big load to drop off. Just another forty miles and he's there."

"The highway," Kim said. "A trucker. Is that what you're seeing, Shelby? A trucker? Panos, Sparrow is in the van near the edge of the parking lot. Right by the bend in the highway and the edge, before the cliffs."

"It's hard to keep his eyes open. Just a

second. Just one tiny wink of sleep."

The music in the club was loud. The sound of metal on metal and brakes from a semi-truck was louder. Without thought, Shelby cupped her mouth and ran for the door, slamming into people and not caring. She burst through the doors and watched in horror as a huge tractor trailer truck flipped onto its side, jackknifing as it careened into the parked black van. It and the van went barreling towards the guard rail and the cliff. A ball of flames engulfed the van and truck cab.

Vaguely, she heard someone screaming and realized it was her. She ran directly at it all, yelling for her brother the entire way. Strong arms lifted her, keeping her from getting closer and another boom went off, rocking the entire parking lot.

She kicked and tried to break free of the iron-clad hold but it was pointless. Kim and Panos ran towards it all. Additional men joined them, trying and failing to get closer to the wreckage. People from the club poured out and into the parking lot, leather-clad and trying to help as well.

There was movement to the far left of the wreckage area. The others were focused on the main portion. The figure was as massive as Aeson and was dragging something.

Two somethings to be exact. One in each hand.

Turning, she stared up into Aeson's face. When she realized it couldn't be him, she gasped. "Shelton!"

Aeson held her tight.

"It's him. It's Shelton. Look!" She pointed and Aeson set her down gently.

Shelby took off in a full run. It wasn't exactly easy to do in heels but she did it all the same. Her brother was shirtless, wearing a pair of soot covered jeans that looked as if they'd been through a war. The men he was dragging appeared to be alive but out cold. He set them down, his gaze finding hers.

She leapt at him and he caught her, hugging her close as she plastered his face with kisses. He chuckled. "Peep," he said, using his nickname for her. "I'm all right. You can stop crying now."

She held him tight, nearly strangling him. He had to pry her off his neck before setting her down. One of the men moaned and looked up, his eyes only partially opened.

Just then, the others all seemed to swarm in on them at once. Panos was there, checking the men on the ground. Kim was doing the same and then joining in to hug Shelton quickly before turning to find another man rushing at them, the zipper to his pants undone.

"I was takin' a piss and—"

"Louis is over here going on about Sparrow having wings." As Panos said it, Shelby tensed, refusing to let go of her brother.

He kissed her cheek and winked, holding her out a bit and looking towards Panos. "I yanked their sorry asses away from the edge," he said.

She heard it then, the semi-conscious detective mumbling about wings. Giving everyone a shit-assed grin, her brother turned, putting his back to them. Huge black wings that spanned the entire width and length of his back were tattooed there. "Yep. I got 'em. You just missed me flying. I looked like Superman or something. I'm awesome like that."

She made a point to not flinch at his wording.

Kim stood back as the paramedics and firemen arrived. She shook her head. "Where the hell is your shirt, Sparrow?"

Shelton motioned to the cliff. "It caught fire. I ripped it off."

Kim shook her head. "Luckiest bastard known to man. When your sister flipped in there and I heard the crash, I thought for sure I was coming out here to hold Shelby back from watching your dead ass get pulled from the mess."

She tensed.

"Yeah, well, you'd have had stiff competition in the holding her back department," Panos said, pointing to something behind Shelby.

She turned and found Aeson there. She smiled and went at him, hugging him too as if she'd known him a lifetime. "He's safe."

"So I see," said Aeson, returning her embrace.

"Who the hell is this douche and why is he touching my baby sister?"

With a sigh, Shelby pulled away from Aeson and looked at her brother. "You were first by like five minutes so stop acting like years separate us."

"You are twins?" Aeson questioned, his accent thickening.

She patted his muscular chest and nodded. "Yes, it's clear to see he took up more room in the uterus though."

Her brother chuckled softly.

Unable to stop herself, she began to cry again.

Shelton tipped his head back, composed himself and then came for her. He had to bend to meet her eye to eye. "Peep, look at me."

She did.

"I made you a promise and I intend to keep it," he stressed. "Didn't I say I'd always be here for you?"

She nodded. "I couldn't see anything past the bad," she whispered, losing her composure again. "I tried but I couldn't see. I should have seen this before. I should have known. I should have told you."

"Peep, you've been under so much stress and I don't expect you to play oracle to me." He looked past her at Aeson. "Hint at all that she's a whack job and I'll shoot you here and now. Understood?"

"Understood," Aeson said calmly.

Shelton took his sister's hand. "Hey, stop. No crying or I'll do stupid things to try to stop it. Remember the time you cried when I fell out of that tree? I ended up singing the theme to the Love Boat to you for an hour just because it made you laugh."

She swallowed hard, nodding. She did remember all the times in their life he'd tried to get her to smile. Shelby tried and failed to control her whirling emotions. She reacted, kicking her brother in the shin as hard as she could.

"Shelby?"

"You big, stupid, idiot! This is all your fault."

He blinked in surprise. "How is this my fault?"

"None of us would be here now if you'd have told me I was dating a sociopath. Shelton Christopher Sparrows, I'm so telling Dad on you."

"What?" he asked, sounding like a child instead of the twenty-seven year old man he was. "Like I wanted that fucker near you? Panos locked me in a cell for the first forty-eight hours of us figuring out who that dick might be. That's two days, Shelby." He put up his fingers for emphasis. "Two days of needing to keep me locked up because I was going to find Roland and kill him."

"So," she put a hand on her hip, "you weren't planning to warn me then? Just off him?"

He tossed his hands in the air. "I surrender. There is no winning with you. Ever. I am the world's worst brother. I get it."

She cried more. "Shelton."

"Yes?"

"I love you even though you're

an idiot."

His voice trembled as he spoke, "I had to sit in that damn van and watch you walk into what I was sure was going to be your death. I don't care how many men we have on this, he's sick and he's smart."

"He's also missing," Kim added from the side. "My guess, he spotted you and realized this had been a trap."

Shelton grabbed for Shelby but looked at his colleagues. "If he knows this was a trap, he won't bother keeping up pretenses for the sake of the thrill kill. He'll go at Shelby full force and when we're least expecting it."

The paramedics tried to get to her brother, wanting to check him over. He waved them away and shook his head. Panos tried to force him to be checked. With a flip of his middle finger, her brother glared at his longtime friend. "Fuck off. I'm fine. Banged up but alive and well. Louis and Phanes are shaken but fine too. Jeps was takin' a piss so he's untouched. The truck driver, he didn't fare as well. Go mommy him. I'm fine. Right now, I'm gonna take my baby sister to my place and refuse to take my eyes off her until that sick son-of-a-bitch is caught."

"I'm not going home with you. You're a slob."

Her brother grinned. "Fine. I'll call Dad. I'll explain everything to him. You can go stay with him. Better yet, he'll come stay with you."

She gasped. "You wouldn't."

"I would."

She cringed. "I'd rather take my chances with a serial killer. Dad will end up taking me and locking me in a tower that no person on Earth can get to."

Shelton laughed, getting the inside joke.

Panos tossed Shelton a set of car keys. "Take the unmarked and get her somewhere safe. Call when you do. And, Sparrow, I'm glad ya got wings, man. I was worried there for a minute."

Shelby grinned at her brother.

Aeson stepped closer. "I will take them where they need to go."

She waited for Panos to protest. He

seemed to consider it before nodding. He put his hand up. "Keys back. Now."

"What?" Shelton questioned.

"Keys."

With a snort he threw them at his friend and then pointed at Aeson. "Fine. But know I'm kicking your ass later for kissing her. Don't think I didn't catch that on the video feed before the whole near death experience."

Aeson appeared amused. "I would expect nothing less from the brother of my woman."

"Your woman?"

"He's in need of mental help," Shelby said, trying to calm her brother. "Can we just go now? I want to get some of my things before I go to your place. Aeson can take us to my house and we can use my car from there."

"You are not taking this guy home with you."

"Why not? He's not a serial killer? Take the fun out of your stakeouts."

Shelton grumbled under his breath. "Fine."

Chapter Five

_____

AESON STARED AROUND SHELBY'S HOME, noting how eclectic her tastes were. He noted something else, from her oversized balcony one of the many portals to his realm was clearly visible. Of course, one could not actually see the portal, but rather sense it. One could see large winged men appearing and seemingly vanishing if one looked hard enough and at the right moment.

From everything Aeson knew the portal in question wasn't heavily traveled because of its close proximity to a densely populated area. Secrecy was important. They dealt with enough "angel" sightings as it was.

Humans nowadays tended to rationalize what they couldn't understand.

Such a simple race of people.

"Shelby," Shelton said, sounding agitated. "Can I get rid of your new buddy here? I think he's more than seen you're here and safe. He's welcome to go."

Aeson didn't comment. He focused his attention skyward, knowing if he had a sister, he'd be much the same way if a male, who was clearly interested, was near.

"Shelby?" her brother repeated, worry creeping into his voice. He went towards the stairs and unease settled over the home.

Aeson was about to go after Shelby himself when she appeared, making no sound. She wore clothing that was designed to be comfortable but still managed to hug her every curve. In fact, it was just as tempting as the baby doll dress had been.

It is not the clothing, he thought. It is her.

"Where the hell is your bag?" Shelton shook his head and went to speak again, but his sister cut him off, putting her hand to his mouth.

She pointed upwards and nodded.

Shelton groaned. "You've got to be fucking kidding me. Really? On top of the night we've already had?"

Shelby's gaze darted towards Aeson as she touched her brother's arm. "Shelton, don't let them see Aeson. Please. The last time they saw a man near me who wasn't related—"

Aeson took a step in their direction. "Who is they?"

"Listen, buddy, your big bad biker dude image may work with the ladies at that club but it's not impressing me," Shelton said. "How about you get in your car and just drive as fast as you fucking can?"

"How about I not," Aeson countered, his patience with the man beginning to wane.

"Aeson, please," begged Shelby, her blue gaze moistening. "Just go. Now."

It would have been easy to take exception to her quick dismissal of him but he picked up on her distress. Her fear.

For him.

"Shelby, speak freely with me. What troubles you?"

Shelton snorted. "Dude, what troubles her is that she knows what's coming will rip you into iddy biddy pieces."

She slapped her brother. "Knock it off. He's seen too much already. He took what I can do in stride. Too well even. He's not once asked me about it and he's not once stared at me like I'm a crazy freak. You will not treat him like this. Am I clear?"

Shelton grunted. "Fine. But if he doesn't go now, I can't be held responsible if they gut him. I mean really now. I think this should be taken as a sign you shouldn't be around him. You meet him while on a date with a killer, I get slammed into by a semi and now..." He glanced upwards.

Shelby grabbed Aeson's hand and tugged, trying to get him to budge. He refused to move, sensing a disturbance.

Others like him were near.

Was Shelby aware of shifters?

Needing to see if she was and if so, what her thoughts on his kind were, he inclined his head and stepped towards the door, his intention to watch over her from a point she could not see.

Shelton took two strides to the door and Shelby gasped. Twisting, Aeson spotted a man on the balcony. He was shirtless and wearing jeans. Upon closer inspection, Aeson recognized the man.

Rhios—a fellow bird shifter.

Shelton grunted. "Shit, Dad, we thought you were someone else."

Dad?

Shelby rushed towards the newcomer, tossing her arms around his neck and hugging him tight. "Daddy."

Rhios returned the hug, lifting her off her feet and kissing her temple. "What has happened?"

Shelton pursed his lips. "Nothing."

"Young man," Rhios said. "I sensed danger clouding over you both on this evening. Do not lie to me." He looked down at Shelby. "You tell me."

She blinked up at him and Aeson

could see the man's hardened exterior melting quickly. "Everything is better now, Daddy. I promise."

"I worry," Rhios said, hugging her again.

"I know."

Rhios glanced in Aeson's direction and the minute they locked gazes, Rhios gasped, jerking his daughter behind him. His large wings unfurled, snapping outwards, blocking Aeson's view of Shelby.

She yelped. "Daddy, no! He can't see this. He can't know."

Rhios nodded to Shelton. "Come."

Shelton eyed Aeson. "Dude, wanna tell me why my dad is flipping out more than you are at the sight of a guy with wings?"

"Shelton, I spoke," Rhios snapped. "Come away from him, this instant."

"Dad, I'm not afraid of some biker dude wanna be."

"Son, should Aeson wish you dead, I fear you and I together might be unable to stop him. He is not a man to be taken lightly and he has witnessed my betrayal of our kind firsthand."

Aeson remained calm. "By betrayal I will assume you mean hiding the fact you have a family in the human realm. You mated with a human woman?"

"She was not my true mate, but I will not apologize for loving her," Rhios said, his head held high. "She gifted me two fine children before her death."

"Daddy?" Shelby asked, her voice sounding so small. "You know Aeson? He's like you?" She peeked out from behind her father's wing.

"I would never harm you," Aeson said.

Rhios snorted. "I know the penalty for betrayal. I will die before I allow my children to be harmed."

Aeson lifted a hand, silencing the man. "Rhios, if memory serves, were you not in command of the sixth legion of men during the Great Wars?"

"I was."

"And did you not sacrifice much to protect our kingdom from our enemies?"

The man nodded.

"Then why would you believe I would order the death of you and your family when you served our people without question or hesitation?"

"But, my prince, it was forbidden to procreate with humans. To taint our line of shifters."

"Prince?" Shelby's eyes widened.

Aeson laughed softly. "Rhios, you really must return home more often. Have you not heard the news? Kabril is mated to a human female. She is queen of our people. They have three fine sons and I suspect more on the way. Sachin too is mated to a human woman. He was blessed with girls. I believe he lives in fear one day Kabril's sons will attempt to woo his daughters."

Rhios drew his wings into himself and shook his head. "The king is mated to a human? Really?"

"Yes."

"And what of you, Aeson?" asked Rhios. "Are you mated as well?"

His gaze went to Shelby. "Soon enough, I will be."

Rhios noticed the action and stepped forward. "You seek my daughter's hand?"

"Of course not," Shelby said. "He barely knows me."

Ignoring her, Aeson focused on her father. "I do. The Oracle warned of danger surrounding her—of pending death should I not find her. It directed me as best it could to where she would be on this night."

"And you are sure the Oracle spoke of my daughter?" Rhios asked.

"The seers rambled about a sparrow, telling me it was representative of her. And they said the Oracle pushed images at them as it would for a fellow seer."

Rhios drew in a sharp breath. He pulled Shelby to him, hugging her again. "I see. I, umm, was not prepared for this day. I have spent so long hiding them among humans I never in my wildest dreams thought she would have a male suitor from our race or that he would be of your standing, Aeson."

"Uh, Dad, you sound like you're actually going to give this dick Shelby." Shelton stepped closer, appearing anything but amused.

"Shelton, Aeson is a prince. Show him respect."

Shelton snorted. "A prince who had his fucking tongue down my baby sister's throat less than an hour ago. And he's not my prince. I'm not one of them, remember? I'm just some half-breed."

Rhios looked to his son. "The only difference between you and the males of our race is that you were not born with the ability to fly. But your wings came to you, Shelton. It took sixteen human years but they came."

Shelby turned her gaze downwards.

Rhios touched her cheek. "Sweetheart, just because you have not the ability to fly, it makes you no less of value to our kind. You are a female seer. Such a thing is unheard of back home. Only males are gifted with such knowledge and foresight into the future. You are a prize indeed. If you do not believe me, simply look upon the man the bird gods selected for you— the man destiny picked to be yours. He is a powerful warrior, Shelby. He is also a prince among our people."

She glanced at him and then leaned towards her father more. "Daddy, I'm not running off into the sunset with him. I only just met him and really, I'm freaking out on the inside about him being like you and Shelton. Oh, and every time you say the word prince, I want to shriek and run in the opposite direction."

Rhios grinned. "I thought all little girls dreamed of growing to wed a handsome prince."

She kissed her father's cheek. "Nope. I used to want to marry a man just like you, Daddy."

Her father turned her to face Aeson. "And you shall."

"Daddy, no, I'm not—"

"Shelton, come," Rhios said. "We will leave them to complete the bonding ritual."

"Dad, you're not fucking serious," Shelton protested. "You're not going to let some random guy who shows up out of the blue marry your only daughter are you? My God, as if this isn't bad enough, there is a serial killer out for her blood. I

73

need to get her to a safe place and then I need to hunt him."

"A serial killer?" asked Rhios.

"It's a long story, Daddy," Shelby said.

"Make it short." Rhios crossed his arms over his chest and waited as Shelby told him everything she knew. When she was done, he shot a hard look to Shelton. "And you did not come to me with this information?"

"No. Figured you'd just rip the guy's head off."

Aeson grinned. "I offered to do as much."

Rhios glanced at him. "You will keep her safe from this man?"

"I will."

"Dad?" Shelton asked.

Rhios ignored him. "My prince, she is my only daughter. Your word you will cherish her as she deserves to be cherished and that you will die protecting her should the need arise."

"Rhios, call me Aeson. No titles. Not between family."

"Family?" Shelton groaned. "No one is letting you marry my little sister."

"Shelton, come."

"Dad."

"You have seen how males of our kind will do just about anything to try to have a female of our race?" Rhios lifted his head.

Shelton nodded.

"Imagine that tenfold. That is what Aeson will be like protecting her. It is what a mate does for his significant other. It is primitive, instinctual and he will do it as though he were drawing in air—automatically. Do you not wish to know she is always guarded? That the man she is with can and will kill all who threaten her? That he is able to provide for her and for any children they may have? And most importantly, that he will never look upon what your sister can do as a curse but rather a blessing bestowed upon her by the bird gods?"

Shelton cursed under his breath and dragged his feet on his way to his father.

Shelby grabbed her brother's arm.

"What? No. You can't leave me here with him."

Aeson failed to hide his smile.

"Peep," Shelton said. "Dad is right about this. Trust me when I say I wish he wasn't." He looked to Aeson. "Roland comes anywhere near her and—"

"I will pluck the eyes from his head before I disembowel him slowly, telling him the entire time of his mistake in coming for her. With his dying breath, he will know my woman is not to be threatened. Ever."

Shelton shrugged. "Works for me."

Rhios approached Aeson and they greeted in the way males of their kind did. First they clamped shoulders and then they leaned in, in a hug like manner.

"May the union be blessed," Rhios said.

Aeson kept hold of the man. "With your permission, I would like to take Shelby home with me."

"I guess it's all right by me but, Aeson, it has to be her choice. Already we take her options from her in regards to you. If there is anything you should know about human women or women who are raised human —they don't take kindly to losing their choices."

"Wise words, old friend," Aeson said, releasing the man. "I will send word regardless so that you do not worry and if I am able to convince her to occupancy me, I believe it would please her greatly for her father and brother to join her there as well."

Rhios grinned as he led Shelton to the balcony. The men shared a look before releasing their wings and taking flight. Shelby squeaked again and backed away from Aeson so fast she nearly fell.

He stayed in place, her antics amusing. "Shelby?"

"What?" she asked, her voice barely there.

"Have you anything you wish to ask of me?"

"After the whole cross thing at the club, I'm terrified to find out anything more. I'm good. You can go now. I'll, umm, call you later."

"I do not have a phone," he said.

She gulped. "I'll write."

"And what post man do you know who would deliver such a letter to me in another realm?"

She touched her throat.

"Do not be nervous," he said. "As I told you earlier, I will allow no harm to come to you and none will do what you wish not to have done. This extends to myself as well. I will do nothing you do not wish to have done."

She seemed to relax slightly but kept her distance. "I'm nervous."

"Do not be."

"I'm not really used to chatting it up with guys who know all my dirty secrets. The men I've met who can shift forms haven't been good men."

"There are many of us, Shelby. It stands to reason a number of our kind would be unsavory. Is that not true of humans as well?"

"I guess," she said.

"Tell me something."

She perked.

"When I touched you, you felt the connection between us, yes?" he asked.

A hand went to her hair. She twirled it absently. "Yes."

"Did you not enjoy the feeling?"

"I did."

"And answer me this—when you felt threatened by your date, what did you do?"

She was quiet a moment before looking directly at him. "I stayed close to you."

"And when you were celebrating your brother being unharmed..."

"I went directly to you," she finished. Shelby took a step closer to him. "You're pointing out how even though I only just met you, I'm drawn to you and that I trust you on some baser level."

"Yes."

"Because of the destiny thing?" she inquired.

"I believe so, yes."

Chapter Six

SHELBY BIT HER LOWER LIP, MOISTURE welling in her eyes.

The sight did him in. He moved quickly to her, pulling her into his embrace as she broke down sobbing. Aeson wasn't sure how to respond. The thought of being his mate pushed her to this point.

Shelby trembled in his arms, holding tight to him. "Aeson, this night has been a nightmare."

He stiffened.

She lifted her head, her gaze meeting his. "All but the parts with you."

Unable to help himself, Aeson lowered his head, his lips finding hers. She resisted only slightly before her tongue greeted his.

Aeson's body stirred to life, his cock hardening. He wanted this woman. Wanted to push her against the wall and fuck her until she too admitted she desired him equally.

He drank from her sweet lips as he dragged her against him. She trembled in his arms, her body pressing tighter to his. It was a sign of surrender. He dragged his hands over her shoulders and down her arms before stopping at her hips. He squeezed them, grinding his body against hers as he continued to kiss her.

Shelby held the sides of his face, whimpering as she returned each of his kisses. He was surprised at her level of passion. She was timid yet fiery all in one. It was much welcomed.

Aeson eased a hand down her more, resting it upon her bare thigh. Her flesh was warm to the touch and silky smooth. His cock beat at his trews, wanting free. Wanting in her. Shelby tipped her head and he kissed her neck, his hand skimming over her thigh, easing up to her panty line. She stiffened briefly and he waited for a sign it was all right to proceed.

She surprised him by putting her hand over his and lifting her panties open to him. Aeson smiled against her neck as he trailed kisses over her. He slipped two fingers into her panties and was greeted instantly with heat and moisture.

Shelby ran her hand over his abs and to the top of his pants. She tugged and unlaced the front of them as she moaned lightly. "Aeson," she whispered, her fingers entering the top of his pants.

There was nothing between her fingers and his cock. Her fingers skimmed his distended flesh and he nearly came then and there. He jerked as she wrapped her hand, as best she could, around his dick. She squeezed and then drew her hand up, seeming taken with the head most of all.

Aeson stroked the pad of her pussy. He eased open her slit and pressed a finger into her heat. He met instantly with resistance and halted at once. "Shelby?"

She rocked in place, her gaze hooded as she stared up at him, her hand still wrapped partially around the head of his cock. "Hmm?"

"You are untouched."

"Yes," she whispered before kissing his chest.

He caught hold of her, moving his hand from her panties at once. He would not take her like a savage in this manner. He would make their first joining memorable and as perfect as she was.

She whimpered as he eased her hand from his cock. He chuckled. "Trust when I say it hurts me more to stop than it does you, my sweet sparrow."

She leaned against him. "Aeson, touch me."

He stiffened. "I will. You have my word but not here. Not like this. I shall take you to my home. We will explore every inch of one another there, Shelby. And when you gift me your maidenhood, I will assure it is with the layer of protection—me claiming you as my mate."

She pushed gently on his chest. "No. No claiming me. Not yet. We need time to get to know one another."

He grinned. "We shall know every inch of one another before the night is out."

She groaned. "That's not what I meant and you know it."

"So, you wish for me to promise to take your maidenhood but not your freedom?" he asked, amused with her reasoning.

"Yes."

He had no intention of honoring that wish. "Very well. We shall speak no more of it at the moment. Let us prepare for travel. Yes?"

She tugged at her lower lip. "You mean to the bird realm?"

He nearly corrected her terminology for it but decided against it. "Yes. Have you ever been there?"

Her eyes widened. "Oh, no. Daddy used to tell us stories about it but he's never ever taken us there. Well, he almost did once when I was little and got really sick. He couldn't take me to the doctors here. He nearly took me back home, to your realm, to your healers. He was afraid it would mean our deaths."

Aeson touched her cheek. "I wish I

had known you then. I would have talked him out of such nonsense."

"So, you're saying when I was little, had he taken me home to your healers, no one would have punished him for having an affair and children with a human woman?"

Aeson thought more upon it. "In truth, our minds had not yet been opened to the idea. But, that being said, we would have been so taken aback by children, even children of mixed lineage, that we would have found it in our hearts to welcome you all."

She gifted him a smile. "Can I tell you something?"

"You may tell me anything you wish."

She went to work trying to tuck his long, thick cock back into his trews. He assisted and refrained from commenting since she seemed to be doing it without paying much attention to the action—it was as if she were taking care of him. Like a mate would.

"I have dreams of a place I think might be the bird realm," she said softly. "There is this giant castle that is more browns than grays. Behind it there are moons setting. More than one. I see men flying from the tops of the castle, circling it. There is this large home off to the side." She motioned with her hands, looking far away in thought. "It's made of the same stone as the castle. It's tucked into a bunch of trees, making it hard to see."

Aeson gasped when he realized she was describing his home. She'd had visions of his home?

She lifted a hand. "There is an emblem on the door. It's carved into the wood. A hawk on a coat of arms." She bit at her lower lip more. "There are other small things but that's what I have dreams of most of all. Is it real or did I just imagine it?"

He hooked a finger under her chin. "It is real."

She smiled wider. "It is?"

He dipped his head, kissing her lips gently. "Yes."

"Can you take me there?"

"Of course."

"Now?" she asked, sounding eager.

He chuckled. "First you must change. As much as I enjoy the sight of you in this, it will not work for a long flight. It is cold at that height and I am able to warm you only so much. Since I do not believe you are able to regulate your body temperature on your own, we should assure you are dressed warmly."

"Aeson, how do I pack for going to another realm? And where in the world would I even carry a bag?"

He laughed. "Take only what you wear. I will have dressmakers come to my home and fit you for all you will need while with me. Then, we shall return here and you can decide which items hold most value to you and must come. I have men who will assist in bringing them forth."

She tossed her arms around his neck and squealed. "I'm so excited."

"Then let us find you warmer clothing."

Shelby allowed him to lead her through her home, to her room. It was strange having a man in there, but she overcame the oddness and found a warm sweater, a knit cap and a pair of gloves. She turned to face him and an odd expression came over him. Confused, Shelby tipped her head. "What? What's wrong?"

"You."

She blinked. "Me what? What did I do?"

"You look…"

She blushed. "Like a dork. I know."

He shook his head. "I know not what a dork is. I was going to say, you look beautiful."

She lifted a brow. "Uh, okay. Sure."

Aeson approached and drew her closer to him. "I do not think this will be warm enough for you."

"It's a wool sweater," she protested. "I'll be fine. Promise. Ready?"

He took her hand in his and they made their way down the stairs and to the balcony area. She held up a finger, indicating that he should wait a moment. "I need to set the alarm system."

He perked. "Alarm system?"

"Yeah, you know, an electronic monitoring system that alerts of danger and contacts help if you need it?"

He seemed lost in thought a moment. "Ah, it does what a sentry does?"

"I have no idea what you just said," she commented.

"And now you know how I feel," he returned with wink. He waited as she armed the system and returned to his side. He eased his shirt off and pulled it over her head gently. It was huge on her.

He smiled. "There."

She inhaled. "It smells like you."

"Is that a good thing?"

"Very," Shelby said, blushing more. "What now? When Dad or Shelton carry me they…"

He didn't allow her to finish. He extended his arms and she watched in stunned silence as giant, brownish wings uncurled from behind him. They spanned nearly the width of the balcony. She gulped. Even his wings were huge. She couldn't help but glance downwards, her gaze centering at groin level.

Aeson reached out, hooking her chin

and forcing her to look up. A wicked grin was firmly on his handsome face. "Ready?"

"No." She jerked slightly. "I mean, yes. Maybe."

"Maybe?" he echoed with a laugh. "You amuse me, sweet sparrow." He eased closer to her, his arms going out more. "Come."

She stepped into him, leaning against him. Heat flared through her and she sucked in a big breath, unsure she really was ready to take the plunge with a man like Aeson. He was too much man for her.

"Sweet sparrow," he whispered against her ear. "I can sense your urge to run from me. You would be like prey and me the hunter."

Swallowing hard, she fanned her face with her hand and rethought her sweater choice. At the rate she was going, she'd burst into flames before they even took flight.

Aeson tossed his head back and laughed more. The sound was so purely masculine that Shelby's inner thighs responded. She clutched his arms, digging her nails into them, fighting the urge to open for the man before her. This wasn't like her. She didn't toss herself at men. She was quiet, reserved—a friggin pre-school teacher, not a temptress.

He wrapped his arms around her gently and they launched into the air. Her breath caught. It was far from her first time flying with someone, but this felt vastly different from having her father or brother fly her. The wind bit at her face but she ignored the sting, deciding instead to savor the feel of being in Aeson's arms. She felt safe, secure from the world and its problems.

Safe from Roland.

She stiffened.

Aeson kissed her shoulder. "You are well, sweet sparrow?"

"I'm fine," she said, snuggling against him, enjoying the ride so to speak. "What about you? Are you cold?"

His hand splayed over her lower stomach. He caressed her gently. "I am fine. Thank you for your concern."

Shelby fell silent, enjoying the view as Aeson flew effortlessly high above everything. There was a tiny change in the air pressure around her and for a split second mist seemed to swarm in around them. Fearful he'd crash, unable to see where he was going, she gasped and gripped tightly to his forearm as her back remained against his front.

"Shh," he whispered. "We are passing through the veil. The portal between realms."

"Oh," she mouthed, dumbfounded by the events surrounding her. While her father spoke often of his home realm, he never took her there. The mist cleared and she could scarcely believe what was before her eyes. It was as if she'd been transported in time—to a place where castles thrived and the world's beauty remained untouched by the taint of modern roads and buildings.

"Welcome home, Shelby," Aeson said.

She stared wildly around, trying to see everything at once. She wiggled so much in his arms that she wasn't sure how he didn't drop her. He chuckled, flying in a partial circle for her so she could see more of the realm from above.

"It's… it's beautiful."

"This is just a tiny portion of it. It holds much more hidden beauties," he said, dipping low, heading in the direction of a large brownish colored castle.

She thought for a moment he'd land directly on one of the battlements. He overshot it, continuing onward, just past the castle, to a tiny clearing near a wooded area. He landed flawlessly and set her on her feet gently.

She turned to face him and he took her hand in his. "Let us go to what will be our home."

She yelped.

"Would it scare you less if I referred to it as my home for now?"

She nodded.

He chuckled. "Very well. My home… for now."

Chapter Seven

AESON SENSED THE TOLL flying and the day itself had taken on Shelby. She needed sleep. He knew he should usher her straight to his room, relinquish his bed to her and leave her be. That being said, the flight with her had been sweet torture. Her lush ass had been pressed against his cock the entire way, tempting him, teasing him. Already he was on the verge of exploding. He needed release and as selfish as it sounded, he wanted it to be within her.

He still couldn't believe she was here with him. His mate. In his home nonetheless. He closed his eyes a moment, making a silent prayer to the bird gods for the gift before him. A question formed in Shelby's eyes and Aeson bent, kissing her forehead. "You need rest," he said.

She offered a slow smile. "I need you."

"Shelby?"

"You made me a promise," she supplied. "You said you wouldn't do anything to me that I didn't want done."

He nodded. "And I intend to keep it. Follow me. I will show you to my room. You will rest there. I will sleep in the guest quarters."

She laced her fingers through his. "Kiss me."

"Shelby?"

She exhaled loudly. "Kiss me."

He bent, doing as she wished. Gods above, her lips tasted divine. So sweet. So pure. She would be like heaven when he took her, he was positive of as much. He skimmed his hand down her arm, his tongue still caressing her. She touched his chest, exciting him more. He bent, lifting her in her arms, cradling her to him.

She gasped, their kiss slipping for a

moment as she wrapped her tiny arms around his neck. He stared down at her. "You are not ready for this. For me. For all of me."

"I'm ready," she said.

He was thankful for her response because he wasn't sure he had it in him to wait. With long strides he covered the distance to his sleeping chambers. He used his foot to shut the door behind him. He smiled at her shocked intake of breath. "Still wish for this?"

"Yes."

He eased her onto the large bed and it seemed to swallow her up in its greatness. She stared up at him, her lips too tempting to resist a moment longer. He climbed up and over her, bending and sampling her tender mouth once more. Aeson's breathing was off the charts. It was as if this were his first time bedding a woman. In a sense, it was.

It was his first time with his mate.

The word scattered around in his brain before landing in his chest. It tightened.

He'd gained so much in a day yet now stood to lose even more. Before Shelby, he'd lived each moment by the moment, never caring about the future or what it might hold. Now that she was with him, all that needed to change.

He sighed against her mouth. "Rest, my sweet sparrow."

She tugged at his shoulders, pulling him down onto her more. "Aeson, please."

Shelby lifted her head and captured his mouth with hers. She was possessive in her quest for kisses and Aeson's cock responded at a frightening rate. He eased his body against hers, his covered cock rubbing against her thigh. He wanted in her. Denying it was pointless. He shifted more on her, his swollen cock pressing to her mound. There were too many clothes between them. Too much material. He began yanking, pulling, shredding everything between him and his prize.

Shelby.

She squeaked, arching her back to him, her eyes wide. She bit at her lower lip, nodding, helping him remove the last of her clothing. She lay beneath him, fully exposed and his breath caught. A more beautiful woman he'd never seen. She was his and his alone. He didn't deserve one such as her.

She reached between them, her hand finding his shaft. She eased her fingers around him but they didn't meet. She gasped. "Aeson… you're huge."

A satisfied smile crept over his face. "I am."

"Will it hurt?" she questioned.

"Only slightly, my sweet sparrow."

An expression he couldn't read passed over her. She kissed him again, wiggling beneath him. "I'm ready."

"You are?" he asked, laughing as he ran his hand down the length of her, to her pussy. He touched her slit and found she was indeed ready. Wet and welcoming.

He rubbed her clit and she nearly came straight up and off the bed. She grabbed hold of his shoulders and he eased her legs apart more. He rubbed again and she panted, arching to him, grinding her hips just right.

"Ah, ta'konima," he uttered softly. "I can wait no longer."

"I want you in me."

Aeson lined up the head of his cock with her pink, wet entrance and stared down at her a second before he thrust in, going to the hilt.

She whimpered slightly and then her lips found his. She rotated her hips under him, his cock deep within her.

He knew he should stop, pull out and return to this when it was more romantic for her, but he couldn't stop himself. He began pumping in and out of her tight body, slowly at first.

Shelby's fingernails dug into his back, stinging. The pain encouraged him to be more aggressive with her. He rode her harder, faster, until she was panting wildly beneath him. Her legs wrapped around his waist and she continued to dig her nails into his back. There was a half second of additional pinching, low in his back before Aeson lost control and his wings emerged. They sprung out, flapping madly as he pumped like a depraved man into his mate.

Shelby's eyes widened and she reached up, stroking his wings tenderly, driving him even madder with lust and blind need. Aeson lost it, his cock twitching as seed erupted from him. He stayed rooted in her, unable to move. She was divine. Heavenly in her acceptance of him.

Shelby continued to stroke his wings as she lay under him. He let out a shaky breath. "Did you come?"

She tipped her head. "Hmm?"

"My sweet sparrow, did your body find release as well?"

"It hurt but in a good way," she returned.

He knew then she had not orgasmed. He stayed in her, his cock still hard. Reaching down, Aeson tweaked her clit, rubbing it just so. She jerked and gasped. "Oh, Aeson. Oh!"

He grinned. "Do you accept me—all of me from now until the end of time?"

She wriggled and wraggled beneath him, thrashing about wildly. She heaved long breaths as she grabbed his upper arms. "Oh, Aeson."

"Do you accept me—all of me from now until the end of time, Shelby Sparrows?"

"Yes," she returned. "Yes I accept you. There. Right there."

With that, he pushed deep, plowing his cock into her tight, soaked pussy. His magik wrapped around them, sharing his essence with her, his life force and his longevity. She would now live the life of an immortal. She was his for eternity.

Shelby cried out and he moved his hand from her cunt. He fucked her with intensity, finding pleasure in his mate's body. His magik doused them with static-charged energy. Shelby either didn't notice or didn't care. She kissed him and he lost himself in her. There was no denying it now. Shelby was his wife—his mate—his only woman.

The very thought did him in. He jerked, releasing in her once again, soaking her womb with his seed. With long, heavy breaths, he put his forehead to hers.

She giggled softly. "I'm pretty sure I came that time."

He laughed. "I would agree."

She locked gazes with him. "Aeson."

"Yes?"

"Promise me something."

He kissed the tip of her nose. "Anything."

"Promise you won't just claim me without my permission. Promise you'll give us time to get to really know each other. Time to be a couple before you make me your wife. I sort of understand about it all. My father explained it to me a little."

He stilled.

She didn't know? The act was already done. The claim was already staked and accepted on her part. She was already his wife. There was no taking it back.

Panicked, Aeson nodded. "Y-yes. Of course, my sweet sparrow. I promise."

She smiled and then kissed him. Her nose wrinkled. "It's really, really wet down there."

"Then let us bathe, dry you and then make you wet again."

She laughed as he exited her body before lifting her and carrying her towards his personal bathing chamber. Guilt ate at him with each step he took. He wasn't sure how he was going to explain to her that it was too late—she was already claimed.

Chapter Eight

SHELBY LAUGHED AS AESON TUCKED A flower behind her ear. He took her hand back in his as they walked along a wooded path. The realm was beautiful. It was so untouched by what took from Earth's beauty—the industrialism and technology—that she couldn't stop staring and noting the absence of things like paved roads and skyscrapers.

It was perfect.

Being here with Aeson was even better.

She giggled and went to her tiptoes, kissing him sweetly.

He wagged his brows and drew her against his body. "Mmm, continue and I will be buried deep within you again."

She gulped. She was sore from their night of lovemaking.

Aeson laughed, touching her cheek gently. "Worry not, my sweet sparrow. I know you came to my bed untouched, and I understand your body needs time before I can ravish it more."

She tugged on his shoulders, forcing him to bend so she could kiss him again. "You're so cocky."

He tongued her mouth. "What of my cock?"

"Aeson," she chided. "You're terrible."

"I know. Perhaps you should take me home and punish me. With your mouth please."

She thought about having his large cock in her mouth once more and she blushed.

He tilted her chin upright. "What happens between us is beautiful, sweet sparrow. Never question that. Never doubt it. Never, ever be ashamed by it."

"Easy for you to say. You're a seasoned pro," she murmured. "My experience consists of last night."

"You have me at your beck and call, Shelby," he said with a grin. "Have you need of tutoring in the finer arts of sex, you have but to ask. Though, you should know, I find myself so lost in you that I lose focus easily."

"My lord," a man said, rushing up the path. He spotted Shelby and came to a grinding halt.

"Taqeen, speak freely," Aeson said.

The man nodded. "Yes, my lord. Excuse the interruption but a summons has gone out. You have not responded and your brother is worried. He has been most concerned over the welfare of your chosen one." He stared directly at Shelby.

Shelby offered a pensive smile.

The man's demeanor changed somewhat. He returned the smile, seeming less threatening. "Are you she?" he asked.

"She who?"

"His chosen one, of course," Taqeen stated evenly.

Aeson chuckled. "She is. Stop glowering at me. I would not bring a random woman home to meet my family. You have

107

known me all my years, old man. How many times have you seen me bring any woman home?"

"I've seen you a fair number of times in the brothels and associating with the likes of the loose morals women," Taqeen said. "This one is a good girl. I can sense it on her. I wanted to be sure she was your chosen and that you did not simply pluck a darling from the sky and demand she come with you. It does seem a very you thing to do."

"Actually," Shelby said with a snort. "He kind of did do that. But, I'm glad he did."

"He's been kind to you?" the man asked.

She nodded. "Very."

"And he's not harmed you? Mind you, Aeson is a good boy but has taken some questionable paths in his young life."

"Young life?" she echoed.

"He is nearly one thousand cycles," Aeson said lowly.

She sucked in a large breath. "Wow,

you don't look a day over forty earth years."

Taqeen chuckled. "I like her, Aeson. Cause her harm or sadden her and I will run you through with the very sword I trained you with. Understood?"

"Of course." Aeson lifted Shelby's hand and pressed a gentle kiss to the back of it. "Taqeen, please notify my brother that I've retrieved my mate and that she is safe and well."

"And is she…?"

Aeson nodded. "She is."

With that, Taqeen headed back down the path.

Shelby twisted in Aeson's arms. "I'm what?"

"In need of food," he said, turning her in a circle. "Come. I shall take you home and fill your belly with food and then with my seed, yes?"

She laughed as she sank against his embrace. "You're too much. You really, really are."

"So I have been told."

She grunted. "Put me down."

"I rather like holding you."

———

AESON CHUCKLED at the annoyed grunt that fell free from his mate. She was precious and his. He had yet to tell her that he'd done the one thing she'd asked he not—claim her. She would come to love him with time. He was sure of it and by claiming her, he added a layer of protection over her. Her life span would extend to mirror his own. She would not age. She would not die.

Since she wasn't entirely human she would have aged slower than most, but without the ability to shift forms, she would have indeed aged. Now, she would not. In addition, claiming her gave him the ability to track her and to sense her emotions better. Should she ever be in danger, he would know. Gods help any who attempted to harm her.

His grip on her tightened as he thought of various scenarios where Shelby might be injured or harmed.

She gasped. "Too tight, Aeson."

He cleared his head. "What?"

She pushed at his arm. "You're holding me too tight."

"My apologies," he whispered, kissing her ear. He headed quickly back to his home and the moment the door shut behind them, Aeson set her down, positioning her with her back to his front. He lifted her skirts and slapped her ass playfully.

Shelby laughed and sank back against him. "Aeson?"

"I need to be in you," he said in a hushed whisper.

She nodded. "Yes."

Reaching down, he freed himself from his trews and lifted her off the ground enough to line up with her core. He pushed on her back, bending her over more before stepping to the chair back for extra support. Shelby leaned over it as Aeson pressed the head of his cock into her wet entrance. Her pussy seized hold of his cock and he slid home, going deep, making her cry out. She fit him like a glove and he held his breath a moment, fighting off the need to release in her.

She panted, grabbing hold of the chair back. "Harder."

He nodded, pumping in and out of her harder. His balls slapped against her, making a loud sound, but Aeson ignored it, too focused on how good her pussy felt to care much beyond that. He plowed his cock into her, causing the chair to slide across the floor. He walked with it, never leaving the sanctuary of Shelby's glorious body. When he could no longer hold off the pending orgasm, he reached around, finding her clit with his finger and rubbed it. Shelby cried out, her pleas a mix of wanting him to stop and keep going as if she wasn't sure what she wanted.

Manly victory assailed him as her pussy held firm to him, contracting, pulsing around his cock as she came. He rooted in place, his cum bursting free of him and bathing her womb. He took measured breaths as he leaned over his wife, kissing her shoulder, his cock still twitching in her. "A man could die a thousand deaths in you."

She looked over her shoulder at him. "Is that a good or bad thing?"

"Mmm." He kissed her lips. "It's a very good thing, my sweet sparrow. We must clean and ready ourselves for the feast I am sure my brother is already ordering in honor of us."

She wiggled on his cock. "But I want to play more."

He groaned, wanting the same as her. "Let us see to my brother's wishes and then we shall lock ourselves in our home and not leave for weeks, yes?"

Shelby smiled wide. "Yes."

Chapter Nine

SHELBY STARED BLANKLY AT THE MAN NEXT to Aeson. She glanced at Aeson. "You never once thought to mention you're a twin?"

He shrugged. "We are not."

Kabril grinned. "There is another. Keonae. He too matches us."

"You're a triplet?" she demanded of Aeson.

He nodded. "You are a twin."

"A fraternal twin. Not identical."

"Good thing," he returned. "Shelton is not my type."

She groaned. "Aeson, really. You never once thought to bring this up? You asked me all about my past, what it was like growing up the way I did and about things Shelton and I used to do when we were little and when I asked you about your family, you said—it's large."

"It is."

Kabril nodded in agreement. "It is."

"Oh, sweetie," a woman said as she entered the room. She went right to Kabril and he kissed her temple. "You're fighting a losing battle if you want information from them. They've been alive so long that they tend to not stop and think. They just assume the information is common knowledge or that it's not interesting enough to share. Ask them about battles. They'll never shut up."

Kabril laughed and kissed her again. "Are we truly that bad, wife?"

Wife?

Shelby smiled. "You must be Rayna. Aeson was kind enough to mention you were human. I think he only told me so I'd feel less alone here."

Rayna nodded. "But, I'm told you're a blending of both."

"More human than not, I'm afraid. I

can't fly. My brother can. Daddy says there isn't a difference between Shelton and the males of the race anymore. But me, he tends to avoid discussing much of because he knows deep down I'm very different from the females."

Rayna moved towards her and put out her arms. "Welcome home, Shelby. Kabril and I are so happy you're here. Aeson is so incredibly lucky and I think he knows it. The castle has been abuzz with talk of them seeing him picking flowers and laughing. Two things they aren't used to seeing from him at all. They're already hoping you soften his rough exterior."

Before Shelby could answer, the door burst open and three little boys, all looking exactly alike, came bounding through. They were chasing one another and an older woman came in behind them, looking tired. The boys went wild.

Kabril clapped his hands and instantly, they stopped and froze in place. Their little lips pursed. "Hi father," the one in the middle said.

The one on the end grinned. "Mother."

Rayna gave them a stern look. "Boys, are you misbehaving?"

They shook their heads.

Shelby couldn't help but laugh.

All eyes came to her. The boys' jaws dropped. The one to the end wagged his tiny brows while the one in the center batted his lashes.

Kabril tossed his head back and laughed. "Brother, I dare say my sons have taken a liking to your woman."

The middle one puffed his chest out. "She is too pretty for Uncle Aeson."

Rayna and Shelby laughed.

Shelby bent to be eye level with the boys. "And you lot, how old are you?"

They each held up four fingers.

"I see. So, you're quite old, indeed. Nearly ancient."

They beamed.

She pursed her lips. "Tell me, at your old age, do you find you need to nap to keep your strength up?"

The woman in the doorway sighed.

"My lady, I was trying to get the boys down for their naps but they refused. The young princes have a great deal of energy."

Shelby looked at each of them. "Is that true? Did she try to get you down for a nap but you refused?"

They hung their heads in shame.

"There's still time to prove what good little princes you are," she said, touching one of their shoulders. "What if we make it a race? Who can be first to their bed? First to fall asleep and then who can sleep the longest? I wonder?" She touched her chin. "This may be too much for you. At only four years each, hmm?"

"I shall win," the middle one said.

"No. I will."

"No, me!"

They bolted from the room and the woman at the door looked to her. "You're a mother then, I see?"

Sadness shrouded Shelby. "No. I went to school to teach little ones. Their age actually and slightly younger."

"You've none of your own?" the

MANDY M. ROTH

woman asked. "Really? You're so good with them. A natural."

"If it were possible, I'd have a houseful of my own," Shelby said. "But it's not, so I take pleasure in helping to teach other people's little ones. I have stickers at my house that I use with the little ones I teach. I'll bring them back and give them to you. When the boys do something very good, place a sticker near their name on the chart I'll make you. When they fill a row, they get a treat. Something they really enjoy—be it a sweet, extra play time, whatever. It should help to cut down on the number of escapees you have at nap time."

"Bless you, child," the woman said. "You were sent by the bird gods, for sure."

She left and Kabril and Rayna looked at her. Rayna smiled past her at Aeson. "Hear that? She wants a house full. You better explain to her that the males determine how many children are in a womb at a time—not the female. I know I was surprised when I learned."

Shelby stiffened. "I'm not having children with Aeson."

Aeson touched her shoulder. "We can speak more of them later—in private."

"Aeson," she said, refusing to look at him. "I can't have children. Daddy explained it to me when I was young."

Rayna stepped closer. "And what did your father say?"

"That my mother died while giving birth to Shelton and I. That I couldn't ever have a child with a human male because of the risk that the child would develop traits of the bird shifter and that I couldn't ever have a child with a bird shifter male because I was more human than not and like my mother, my body wouldn't be able to handle the stress."

"Surely he did not mean you could not have children with your chosen mate," Kabril said. "Rayna was fully human when I mated with her. She carried the boys with ease. As did Paige with Sachin's young ones."

"Daddy mentioned true mates before. He said my mom wasn't his but that he'd somehow been blessed with Shelton and me. He kind of feared that like my mom, I'd be able to get pregnant from any male —not just my chosen or whatever it is you call it. And that my body would suffer because of it."

Rayna stared at Aeson. "What does your gut tell you?"

Kabril laughed. "He hopes no children come of their union. See the way he looks at the boys. I think he fears them."

Aeson pulled Shelby against him. "My gut tells me when the time is right, we will be gifted with new life and that Shelby will be safe, so will the babes."

She glanced back at him. "You'd have to claim me first and remember, you agreed to give me time to think about it all?"

Kabril coughed.

Aeson shook his head, staring at his brother.

"She does not know?" Kabril asked.

"Know what?" Shelby asked.

Aeson sighed. "Shelby, about the me claiming you."

She paused. "Aeson, you didn't."

There was a pensive shimmer in the depths of his eyes. "I did. In my defense, I couldn't help myself."

She gasped. "Aeson, you promised!"

"I know but you are hard to resist, my sweet sparrow."

She poked him in the chest. "Don't you sweet sparrow me. You are so in trouble right now."

He hung his head like a scolded child, reminding her of his nephews. "Yes, wife."

She jolted at the word wife and he snickered. Shelby smacked his chest. "You are sleeping alone tonight and probably tomorrow night too."

His eyes widened and the smile faded from his face. "But, Shelby…"

Rayna laughed. "Oh, Kabril, look. They remind me of us when I'm mad at you."

"How do you not kill him if he's anything like Aeson?" Shelby demanded.

Rayna snorted. "It's hard. Wish I could say it gets easier with time but they're a stubborn lot. What do you say we go get ready for the feast this evening and leave these two to think about how to behave?"

The king blinked. "I did not misbehave. It was my brother."

"Oh, I'm thinking you've done something I just haven't learned about yet," Rayna said.

"I would never," Kabril said, a sly grin on his face.

"So that wasn't you who was sparring with one hand tied behind your back earlier today?"

He gulped. "N-no."

Aeson laughed.

Shelby pointed at him and he shut up.

Rayna looped her arm through Shelby's. "Let's go."

"Sounds like a plan."

Chapter Ten

Aeson landed gently with Shelby on the balcony of her Earth home. He didn't like the fact they were back, but he'd promised her he'd bring her home long enough to gather what she wanted most. Several guards had come with them. They landed on the balcony as well and Aeson twisted enough to face them. "Check the dwelling first. Assure it is safe."

With a nod, they headed into the home and a few minutes passed before they returned. "Prince, it is empty."

"My thank you," he said, releasing Shelby enough to permit her to walk on her own.

She snorted. "Are you planning to be

this overprotective the rest of our lives?"

"Yes," he responded evenly, taking her hand in his as he entered the home. He led her in and ignored her tiny grumblings about his need to "assert his manhood". She would never understand that it was inborn in him—the fierce need to assure his mate was safe and protected, regardless.

He dipped his head and kissed her quickly, stopping her tantrum before it could become full-blown. She smiled up at him shyly, and he thought about her lips wrapped around his cock. Her brow quirked.

"Stop thinking dirty thoughts."

"I am... not?" he said, clearing his throat.

She laughed and released him. "My brother said he and Dad packed my bags and put them on my bed. Can you bring them down?"

"Of course. You will remain here?"

She nodded.

Aeson went up the stairs and stopped when he entered her bedroom. There were bags upon the bed, but they were opened and everything was thrown about. Rhios was a soldier and it was against his very nature to be so messy. Aeson's hackles rose. Something was wrong. He spun and shouted, "Shelby!"

He ran, missing a number of the steps and hitting the wall in his clumsy haste to get to his mate. He made it to the main level and spun. Where was she? He spotted his guards on the balcony.

"Where is my mate?"

They twisted, looking at him. "She commanded us here."

"She did what?" he asked, unable to believe what he was hearing.

"She growled when we followed her into the cooking area and said very clearly 'stop following me, go look busy on the balcony or something'."

Aeson blinked in surprise. "And you obeyed?"

"She is our princess," one said matter-of-factly. "We are to obey her orders as if they were yours."

Aeson spun. "Shelby!"

The guards pushed into the room. One pointed to the front door. "She went that way."

"You let her go outside? Alone?"

They froze.

Aeson would deal with them later. He took off in the direction of the front door and the second he thrust it open, he found a white cloth on the ground. He sniffed the air and recognized the scent as something used to render one unconscious. It was similar to oil the healers of his realm used when surgery was called for on a warrior.

He thought back to the mess in Shelby's room and to the cloth before him. "Roland."

For a second he couldn't think, couldn't focus. All he saw was red and all he felt was blind panic. One of his head guards grabbed him, shaking him as if were a mere fledgling.

"My lord!" the guard shouted in Aeson's face.

Aeson stilled. "He has her."

"Who does?"

"A serial killer."

The guards appeared confused. They were not used to human terms.

Aeson paused more. "A person who kills many, over and over again for the thrill of the kill. Innocents. Non-war related."

The men gasped.

He looked to one. "Find Rhios. Shelby told me his address."

"Address?"

"Location within the human realm," Aeson said sharply. "Go quickly!"

———

SHELTON AND RHIS flew close by his side as they neared the location they'd managed to track Shelby to. Aeson landed in a hurry and pulled his wings in. Shelton was going on about the need to be stealth and to assure this was indeed the abandoned home Shelby was being held in. Aeson was out of tact and finesse. He charged forward, striking the old door with one blow, sending it into pieces.

"So much for the element of surprise,"

Shelton said.

Rhios followed close behind Aeson as he entered the dwelling. He sniffed the air and smelled blood.

Shelby.

He followed the scent and demolished another door, this one leading downstairs, to a dungeon of sorts.

"They fly, Shelby," Roland said, his voice filtering through the level. "I saw them. They have wings!"

He found a back room and saw Roland there, knife in hand, waving it around madly near Shelby who was chained to a wall. She was limp and bloody.

Roland back handed her. "Tell me of the flying men, bitch!"

"You wish to know of me. I will show you!" Aeson shut off as he went at the man responsible for harming his woman.

———

SHELBY LIFTED her head to the sounds of shouting and commotion. She was partially out of it still but knew enough to understand Roland had taken her from her front porch. She tugged at the chains binding her wrists.

She focused and what she saw ripped a scream from her. Aeson was there, holding Roland off the floor by his neck. Her father was suddenly next to her, grabbing her face.

"Look not at him, Shelby," her father said.

She couldn't look away.

Aeson tore Roland's head clean off, making the act look effortless.

Shelton and the other men grabbed Aeson, yanking him back from the clearly dead Roland. Blood was everywhere. Shelby knew she was still screaming but couldn't seem to stop herself.

Shelton caught Aeson before he could get to her. "You're covered in Roland, man. Go upstairs and wash off."

"She needs me," Aeson said, his gaze locking on her.

Shelby managed to calm somewhat as her father broke the chains holding her. Her father caught her, holding her to him.

She sank into his embrace and closed her eyes. Everything hurt. Roland had hit and kicked her, demanding answers to what he'd seen while stalking her—the bird men.

She came to slightly at the sound of Aeson demanding his wife be handed over to him.

"She is safe with me," her father said, carrying her as if she were a child.

"She... I swore to protect her," Aeson said, sounding as if he were crying. That couldn't be. Her fierce warrior, her stoic prince, her master of the hunt wouldn't break down in tears, would he?

She lifted her head, getting her one good eye open to see Aeson on his knees, his men surrounding him, none saying a word as the hulk of a man did indeed sob.

"My wife was harmed and I did nothing to stop it." He pounded his chest.

"You tore the dude's head off," her brother said from the sidelines. "Not to mention you tracked my sister's location and that means that sick fuck had her less than twenty minutes. With the drive time he had her alone for less than ten minutes."

"Enough time for him to hurt her," Aeson said, still breaking down.

Shelby reached for him. "Aeson."

He shot to his feet, coming for her. "My sweet sparrow. I am unworthy of you."

"Shut up and carry me home. I want a bath. I think I have dead guy on me."

Aeson stilled. "Shelby?"

She leaned and he took her from her father.

"You do not hate me?" Aeson asked.

"No. I love you. Take me home to the bird realm."

"It's not called the bird realm," a guard said.

Aeson shot him a daring look.

The man raised his hands. "Bird realm it is then."

Aeson kissed her temple lightly. "My sweet sparrow, you are my light, my heart, my love."

She began to nod off again. "You love me?"

Chapter Eleven

AESON SAT QUIETLY IN THE HALL OUTSIDE of the room holding his wife. Three days had passed since they'd returned to his realm with an injured Shelby. Three days of healers at her bedside around the clock, speaking things such as bleeding on the brain, internal injuries and what not. Three days of Aeson praying to every bird god he could think of for her to recover and not to leave him.

Rayna exited the room that held Shelby and the healers. Aeson, Shelton and Rhios all stood quickly. It was Aeson who got to the queen first. "How is she?"

"Banged up but fine."

"Did he…?" Shelton asked, his question left hanging. All knew what he was asking. Had Roland raped Shelby?

Rayna shook her head. "No. The sight of Aeson and his men arriving with Shelby, flying, halted that plan, I'm sure. Shelby said he knocked her out with something but that she wasn't totally out of it. My guess is the fact she's part shifter, it didn't work as the sick bastard thought it would. She said she was aware the entire time and no, he didn't rape her. He did hit and kick her though. A lot."

Aeson's gut clenched. He bowed his head.

Rayna touched him. "She said she knew you'd come for her. That her prince would find her." Rayna stared him over. "You need a bath and a shave."

Aeson ignored her. "She is awake? I wish to see her. If one more healer orders me out of the room——"

"Brother," Kabril said, coming around the corner. "Have we not had the talk about you threatening the healers?"

He pointed to the room. "My mate is alert and they continue to thrust me out of the room with their spells and magiks."

Rayna laughed. "Because you hover and bark orders at them."

"She is my wife. I will order…"

"Shut up, already!" Shelby yelled. "My head is pounding and you're not helping it. Stop belly aching and get in here before I pay these healers to zap your butt out of the castle."

Rayna and Kabril laughed.

Rhios touched Shelton's shoulder. "Sounds like she'll be just fine."

"Yeah, Peep is pissed." Shelton looked to Aeson. "Good luck, man. You're gonna need it around her."

The healers exited the room and came straight for the queen. "My lady," one of them said. "She requires rest. Not visitors."

"You're still angry with Aeson for calling you a one-trick healer," Rayna said calmly. "Besides, shouldn't he be with her so she can share the news you only just gave her?"

"News?" Aeson asked. "Is she dying? Oh Gods Above, no!"

Rayna rolled her eyes. "She is not…"

Aeson charged past the queen and into the room. Shelby was sitting up on the bed. "You are not permitted to die!"

She grunted. "Are you about done acting like a fool?"

He paused. "Are you not dying?"

"I'm pregnant. Not dying."

"Pregnant?" he managed as the room began to spin.

Rhios was suddenly there, helping to hold him up. Kabril was forced to lend a hand. Kabril chuckled. "Congratulations, brother. You are to be a father. May you be as blessed as our father was."

Aeson's gaze whipped to his brother. "You wish to curse me with eight sons?"

Kabril laughed. "Oh, yes. I do."

THE END

NOTE TO READERS: Author recommends reading Rise of the King next for max reading enjoyment. Buy Link for Rise of the King

Complimentary Material

The following material is free of charge. It will never affect the price of your book.

Rise of the King Blurb

Rise of the King (King of Prey)
Book four in the King of Prey series.

Warrior, bastard, outcast, traitor to his
kind, these are all labels Lazar has worn
for the past several years, since he took a
stand against the actions of a mad king.
He's defended the Kingdom of the Hawks
even though the blood of the Falcons runs
through his veins. He's bedded their
women, drank their mead and protected
their king. None of that makes him one of
them. An empty pit has been in his
stomach for years, believing his true mat :
perished long ago. When he learns she's

alive, he has to not only win her over, but also make her understand men who can shift into birds aren't the things of nightmares. They're real, and he's one of them.

Sabrina lives a relatively sheltered life. Her overprotective uncle means well but can sometimes go too far. When he shows up with a sexy hunk she's dreamed about, it's all Sabrina can do to control her emotions. As old lies are uncovered, she has to decide if she should open her heart to a man who has made using women an art form and who also happens to have wings. Plus, he's more than just any old shifter male. He's the rightful king of the Falco, and it's time he rose to his position and accepted his destiny, even if that destiny includes her.

Click to buy Rise of the King **today!**

Excerpt: Rise of the King

CHAPTER ONE

ACCIPITRIDAE REALM

The sun, near setting, edged over the crenels of the castle walls. Each gap let the sun's rays shine through directly into Lazar's eyes. He took a moment to adjust to the change in light levels. The pattern the rays cast onto the training yards was captivating.

Lazar pushed his hair from his face and spun, bringing his sword up to block his opponent's strike. The shock reverberated through his arms. His muscular, trained body absorbed it with relative ease. The blow was hard and no practice weapons were used, so steel-on-steel sounds echoed throughout the training yard.

Since they were but fledglings, the bird shifters' males practiced with real weapons. No sense learning if what you were learning with could no more hurt an insect, let alone protect you. As they'd grown into fierce adult males, they'd only perfected the art of battle and swordplay. They conditioned many hours, never allowing their skills to waver. One never knew when one would require them.

The man coming at him had oddly become something of a friend over the course of Lazar's last several years within the Kingdom of the Hawks. Sachin, once someone Lazar would have seized the moment to kill rather than train alongside, turned lightly on his feet, moving with the grace of a true warrior. Lazar drew upon his abilities as a seasoned fighter and twisted, going at his opponent. He nicked Sachin's arm. Something that didn't happen often.

Sachin raised a brow, and a mischievous grin slipped over his face. His amused silver gaze locked on Lazar. "Good one."

"Are you bleeding?" a shrill, feminine voice demanded from the sidelines, interrupting the sparring.

Wisely, both men lowered their weapons as Sachin's mate, Paige, approached the training yard. She eyed her husband and pointed to his upper arm. The tiniest trickle of blood was evident.

It was only a scratch, but from her expression it was life-threatening. "You're hurt."

Sachin scoffed. No man worth his salt would cry foul over a nick such as the one Lazar had given him. It was easy to see the warrior was insulted anyone would attempt to do so on his behalf. That being said, the person doing it was his wife, his mate and a fine balance had to be maintained. "'Tis a scratch, my love."

Paige put a hand on her hip and glared at him, her brown eyes going hard. Her auburn hair spilled over her creamy, pale shoulders. She looked both lovely and slightly like a witch about to cast a thousand poxes upon them all. Lazar guessed the latter, for her temper knew no bounds.

"A scratch, my ass," she sputtered. "You were supposed to be back home for dinner nearly two hours ago, and here I find you horsing around with your buddy and bleeding all over the place?"

It took a moment for Lazar to wrap his mind around all Paige had said. Her human slang often left most of the men of the realm blinking in confusion until they surmised her meaning. Sachin cast Lazar an apologetic look. "It would appear our training has ended for the day."

"You're damn right it's ended," his wife snapped. She was feisty to say the least.

Lazar failed to hide his laughter as the head of the guards took a verbal lashing from a woman nearly half his size. Paige rounded on Lazar. "Think this is funny? Wait until you're mated and we women gang up on you. You won't be snickering then, bucko."

Sachin laughed deeply. "That would be a sight."

Huffing, Lazar puffed out his chest. He had no desire to be stuck with one woman and one woman only. "No offense, but I'd much rather sample many women than tie myself to one."

"Watch what you say in front of my wife," Sachin said sternly. "You will not speak of women with ill reputations before her."

Rolling her eyes, Paige snorted and waved her hand in the air. "Oh please. We all know Lazar's reputation with the ladies —if you can call them that. And I'm hardly a blushing virgin anymore."

Lazar wagged his brows, feeling victorious and oddly proud of his reputation.

Sachin jutted out his chin. "I was as you are once, friend. Mark my words. When you meet your mate, everything changes."

Tightness gripped Lazar's chest. His mate had perished over twenty years ago, taking with her his chance at happiness. He plastered a smile to his face, pushing down old feelings of sorrow and regret. They had no place in his life anymore, and there was naught he could do to change the past. It was etched in stone, and he was sentenced to a life without love.

Already his nights were spent dreaming of a woman who did not exist. His days could not be filled with such foolishness as well. The subject wasn't one he'd broach with Sachin or anyone from the Kingdom of the Hawks. It was personal, and it was no use bringing up that which could not be changed. "I am sure you are correct."

Paige shooed Sachin off and followed behind him, continuing to scold him the entire way. Other guards looked away, knowing they'd catch hell from the head of the guards at a later date if they dared acknowledge their commander's humiliation at the hands of his tiny wife.

Lazar debated returning to the castle to search for one of the kitchen maids again. After waking from his erotic dream, he'd sought one out and fucked her. And he'd taken two in the buttery only yesterday.

Slow week.

He rubbed his upper chest, his hands

skimming over the scratch marks the one he'd fucked today had left. They served as a reminder that while the women of the kingdom sought his cock and toned body, they hated what he was—a falcon shifter. The scratches hadn't been made in the height of passion as a sign of a good time had by all, but rather made to spite him, to spit in his face as to what he was—a falcon shifter. Not a hawk shifter—his nemeses for the majority of his life. Sadly, the scratches paled in comparison to the scars he bore. They were recaps of times best not thought upon.

The kitchen maid from earlier had been wild and wanted him for his body and his skilled cock but didn't want the stigma attached to him—enemy, falcon, outsider. The scratches she'd inflicted were all but healed over. The long soak he'd taken in the hot springs had helped, along with washing away her scent. He found it unpleasant, as he did a lot of the females from the region. They weren't *his* kind.

Glancing around the empty training yard, Lazar drew in a deep breath and let his wings emerge. There was the smallest of pinches in his lower back before his huge wings spanned out and around him. He flexed them, enjoying the feeling of being free. Too long he'd gone between flights. He launched into the air—the need to fly out his aggressions was great. The wind whipped past him, lifting his hair and cooling his aching muscles. He closed his eyes a moment, savoring the feeling.

When he finally landed, it was with a grand view of the kingdom. He sat on his haunches, peering out and over the valley below. It was beautiful, as was most of the realm. The buildings were constructed in a way that didn't totally take from the land-scape—unlike the human realm where skyscrapers and pavement appeared to be all one could see for miles and miles. Humans cared little about preserving the beauty around them. They seemed to want things taller, faster, quicker. Nothing was good enough for them, and one day their hunger for more would be their downfall.

The Kingdom of the Hawks was grand, spanning over most of the

Northern Region of Accipitridae. Some of the homes within it had been built around trees. It wasn't unheard of to enter a villager's home to find a large trunk within and ample light streaming in from many an opening. His kind, the bird shifters, didn't like to feel captured or caged within their dwellings. They liked the feel of the sun on their faces and the smell of fresh air.

Not so long ago, he'd thought of the kingdom's occupants as the sworn enemy —the *Buteo Regalis*—the most hated of all the enemies of his kind.

The *Falco Peregrinus*.

He'd once been a proud member of his kind and a fierce warrior for the cause. It was a cause he'd been led to believe was just and true. He should have known better. Everything that had sprung forth from the mouth of the king of the Falco had been a lie, so why shouldn't the truth about the *Buteo Regalis* be as well?

He'd been following the ramblings of a man hell-bent on power and ruling all the realm. Had he stood his ground and fought for his birthright, the Falco wouldn't be feared by all and thought of as the enemy to nearly all the varying kingdoms within the bird-shifter realm. No, Lazar would not have ruled with fear and lies. He would have ruled very, very differently.

Events and circumstances had left Lazar branded a traitor among his people. He clenched his fists, silently swearing to exact revenge on those who had claimed what was rightfully his.

Here, among the *Buteo Regalis*, or more commonly known to humans as royal hawks, he was trusted by the king yet feared and looked down upon by many of the king's subjects. If they knew the truth of who he was, his actual birthright, they'd not only fear him, they'd see him on the end of a pike, rotting, for all to know what they did to those who crossed them.

Until that time came, he would continue to fight for their cause, fuck their women and drink his fair share of their mead. He'd never been able to pass up a good time. That trait was seen as a flaw by many, himself included.

Movement from the village below caught his eye. He tilted his head to watch as a warrior he'd seen at the castle often enough wandered into the darkened woods surrounding the village. He headed in the direction of a portal to the human realm. Curiosity got the better of Lazar, and he remained perched in place, wondering what would make a man act in such a manner, especially considering that King Kabril had yet to lift the bans on traveling between the realms, and Gardelle was certainly a strict follower of Kabril's rules.

Gardelle was one of the few guards at the castle who spoke to Lazar without a touch of malice in his voice. Never did the man mention trips to the human realm, though. Lazar's love of visiting the human realm was well-known. So was his desire to break rules. So far, Kabril had only made a few comments regarding the manner, mostly to warn him against being seen in flying form by humans. It wasn't like the king had much in the way of credibility when it came to the old rule of no contact with humans, since his new wife and now queen to the hawks was in fact human. So was Sachin's wife, Kabril's head advisor. Lazar chuckled as he thought about Paige's hold over the feared head of the guards.

Lazar caught sight of Gardelle through a tiny clearing in the canopy of the trees. When Gardelle shifted forms, allowing his wings to emerge, Lazar did the same. He backed into a recessed area as the warrior flew by heading straight for the portal to the human realm.

Waiting until the right moment, Lazar remained in place until the object of his curiosity passed before emerging from his hiding spot. He took to flight, soaring above the Tocallie Mountain peaks. Gardelle passed through one of the many portals nestled in the serene area, and so did Lazar, careful to keep a reasonable distance to avoid drawing suspicion.

Gardelle traveled far, and since the human realm had already fallen into dark-ness for the night, it was difficult to see exactly where the man was going without following closer. Lazar increased his speed, knowing that as a Falco Warrior, he possessed speed greater than that of any Hawk Warrior. He regained a visual on the warrior, following close, assuming Gardelle would do as many other warriors did when visiting the human realm—stop at the known whorehouses or seedy bars, as Lazar had once heard them called by a human.

All he knew was each time he needed his dick scratched, he simply flew to one of them. The women there always seemed more than willing to serve his needs, and none held what he was against him because they didn't know. To them he was simply a man, not a shifter. Something that was far from the truth.

CLICK TO BUY Rise of the King **today!**

About the Author

Dear Reader

Did you enjoy this title and want to know more about Mandy M. Roth, her pen names and all the titles she has available for purchase (over 100)?

About Mandy:

New York Times & *USA TODAY* Bestselling Author Mandy M. Roth is a self-proclaimed Goonie, loves 80s music and movies and wishes leg warmers would come back into fashion. She also thinks the movie The Breakfast Club should be mandatory viewing for...okay, everyone. When she's not dancing around her office to the sounds of the 80s or writing books, she can be found designing book covers for New York publishers, small presses, and indie authors.

Learn More:

To learn more about Mandy and her pen names, please visit www.MandyRoth.com

For latest news about Mandy's newest releases and sales subscribe to her newsletter: Sign Up For Mandy's Newsletter

Want to see all Mandy's books? Click here.

Printable PDF list of all Mandy's titles: Click here.

To join Mandy's Facebook Reader Group: The Roth Heads.

Review this title:

Please let others know if you enjoyed this title. Consider leaving an honest review on the vendor site in which you purchased this title. Reviews help to spread the word and boost overall sales. This means more books in the series you love.

Thank you!

facebook.com/AuthorMandyRoth

twitter.com/mandymroth

instagram.com/mandymroth

goodreads.com/mandymroth

pinterest.com/mandymroth

bookbub.com/authors/mandy-m-roth

youtube.com/mandyroth

amazon.com/author/mandyroth

Featured Titles from Mandy
M. Roth

The Immortal Ops Series World
Immortal Ops
Critical Intelligence
Radar Deception
Strategic Vulnerability
Tactical Magik
Act of Mercy
Administrative Control
Act of Surrender
Broken Communication
Separation Zone
Act of Submission
Damage Report
Act of Command
Wolf's Surrender
The Dragon Shifter's Duty

Midnight Echoes
Isolated Maneuver
Expecting Darkness
Area of Influence
Act of Passion
Act of Brotherhood
Healing the Wolf
Wrecked Intel
And more to come…

Cozy Paranormal Mysteries
Once Hunted, Twice Shy
Total Eclipse of the Hunt
Don't Stop Bewitching
And more to come…

Tempting Fate Series
Loup Garou
Bad Moon Rising
And more to come…

The Guardians Series
The Guardians
Crossing Hudson
Ruling Jude
And more to come…

The Druid Series

Sacred Places

Goddess of the Grove

Winter Solstice

A Druid of Her Own

And more to come…

The King of Prey Series

King of Prey

A View to a Kill

Master of the Hunt

Rise of the King

Prince of Pleasure

Prince of Flight

Bureau of Paranormal Investigation (BPI)

Hunted Holiday

Heated Holiday

Prospect Springs Shifters

Blaze of Glory

Parker's Honor

Gabe's Fortune

CPSIA information can be obtained
at www.ICGtesting.com
Printed in the USA
LVOW10s1550230518
578229LV00001B/207/P